HOOKED on the BOXER

PIPER RAYNE

"Who knew a bad boy could mend a broken heart?"

What does a girl do after she discovers her fiancé is a cheating bastard?

In my case, I performed the ritual implosion of all scorned women. I drowned my sorrows in cases of white wine, wallowed in gallons of ice cream, and ignited a bonfire to burn away every damn remnant of his existence. Six months later, the only result was a permanent impression of my ass on the couch.

Adventure Dating my friends dared.
A new and exciting opportunity they said.

I thought they were crazy, but I'm not one to back down from a challenge, so I signed up for the entire four-week deal.
That's where I saw HIM. Lucas Cummings. He isn't the classic rich boy I usually end up with. The one whose idea of working up a sweat is waiting for his margarita to be served beachside. Nope. He's a rough and tough bad boy that all fathers warn their daughters about. You know the type. Cocky swagger, chiseled jaw—the 'V'.

SOLD, I said to myself, until I discovered he was so much more than just a BOXER.

Left Hook.
Right to the heart.

HOOKED *on the* BOXER

Dedicated to our faithful unicorns

ONE

MY PURSE TOPPLES OVER the edge of my kitchen table, and my tube of lipstick rolls to my feet as the bags of appetizers drop on the table. I scramble to pick all the items up and place each one in their designated place. Ever since I canceled my wedding to my cheating bastard of a fiancé, my life has lost its usual order.

I glance at the microwave clock, noticing I have five minutes before my two best friends, Whitney and Lennon, will arrive. Wishing I could cancel and plop my ass on my couch to eat all the appetizers I purchased by myself, I pick up my phone, playing the lecture they'd give me in my head.

What am I, crazy? They'll knock down my door.

They have a constant obsession with my happiness since I left Chase, said cheating bastard, at the altar. Actually, we didn't quite make it there. I never did slip into the white Vera Wang dress. I did love that dress. There's another giant check mark on the long list of things Chase fucked up for me.

The doorbell rings and I slip off my heels, scoop them up, and walk to the door.

Lennon barrels through before I have a chance to open it completely, brown paper bags hanging off her arms. Great, another sex toy she wants us to try out. My friend and her dreams of owning a sex toy company, God help her.

"Don't look so pouty. I bear gifts that will erase the douche."

"I'm not pouty, I'm tired," I say, walking toward my bedroom door.

"Tahl, I hate to break it to you, but you've gotten lazy after the douchecanoe debacle. You used to have enough energy for five of me."

"I'm lazy? This from a girl who thinks cleaning her floors is sliding around with paper towels under her feet." I grip my door handle, ready to escape to my bedroom with the hope tonight's halfway over before I emerge. Not because I don't love my friends, but because they've grown tired of my wallowing. With them gone I can stick a spoon in my pint of Ben and Jerry's and watch the Hallmark channel all night long.

"Don't knock it. That shit actually works," Lennon says and drops her brown paper bags onto my kitchen chair.

"I don't care what you do at your apartment, just don't call me lazy." I step into my room.

"That's why you always keep your shoes and coat on when you visit me, isn't it? That's the reason we always have to come over here. You're a control freak, Tahl." Her over-eyelinered eyes widen, taunting me to retaliate, but I'm not in the mood to argue over my obsessive-compulsive ways. There's nothing wrong with organization and cleanliness.

The doorbell rings again, and Lennon's feet are already moving toward the door, so I sneak into my bedroom to change.

My friends. I love them, but I wish they'd leave me the hell alone.

Two minutes later, Lennon's fist bangs on my door. "Get out here, Tahl."

"Give me a second, Jeez." I open the door, and Lennon looks me up and down like we're thirteen and I'm wearing the cat sweater Grandma gave me for Christmas.

"We've given you six months." She shakes her head, continuing to be displeased with my attire, and grabs my elbow, escorting me to the couch.

"You look comfy," Whit says, a smile on her face. Of course she's smiling. She found a man who treats her with respect. She's with the respectable Webber brother who doesn't believe in cheating. Right now I wonder if that's even possible, a man who doesn't want to have his cake and eat it too. I should warn Whit before the knife pierces her back.

What the hell am I thinking? I've seen the way Cole looks at her. Chase never once gazed at me like that.

I look down to my pajama pants and oversized t-shirt. "Thank you, I am."

Whitney nods, her usual permanent smile plastered to her face.

"We'll deal with your wardrobe in a second." Lennon touches my shoulder and quickly retracts her hand. Holding her finger up in the air, she glances over at Whitney, her dark brows drawn. "What is this?"

"Chocolate sauce. I made myself a chocolate malt last night. I forgot this should go in the wash." I scramble to stand up, but Lennon's hand lands on my thigh.

"No, we can burn them later." She peers up and down at me—again.

"You're being bitchy," I say, annoyed. Neither of them has to be here. I'll manage fine by myself.

"Would you prefer me to coddle you?" she says in a sugary-sweet voice.

"Lennon," Whitney warns, and it's clear to me now that they've had conversations about me.

"No, I'd rather Whit cuddle me," I say.

Lennon stands, huffing as she walks over to the table. "Tahlia, you've lost it," she says, walking back with her arms full of the vibrators she's pulled from the bags she brought. I can see now that she has packaging for her product so she must be making some strides with her fledgling business.

"Lennon," Whitney warns her again, but Lennon's not one to shy away from communicating her thoughts.

Understatement of the century.

"No, Whit. We've done it your way for the past six months." Lennon shoots her a look. "We've been dealing with her using a light touch as though she's a hairline fracture away from shattering. She needs a flogger now. Let's call a spade a spade, shall we?"

"Are we playing poker?" I ask, and Lennon's mouth hangs open.

"Look at you, Tahlia." Her hand moves up and down my body.

I don't see the problem.

"You're wearing pajamas that are about five sizes too big and have more stains on them than the blue dress Monica Lewinski wore. You don't answer our phone calls half the time, and you never come out with us. And guess what I found in your sink?" She rushes over and holds up a spoon.

"A spoon?" Whitney asks, and snickers. "And Tahlia's the one losing it," she says, leaning back in her chair, with her cute jeans and t-shirt, looking totally put together.

"When is the last time Tahlia has ever left something in the sink?"

I stand up, beeline it to her and pluck it out of her hand, placing it in the dishwasher.

"I was running late," I say, as my skin itches realizing I forgot to turn the dishwasher on before I left for work this morning.

"Tahl." Lennon's voice lowers and she places her arm

around my shoulder, guiding me to the couch again. "Whitney and I have bought you a gift."

"A gift?" My eyes veer to a smiley Whitney bouncing with anticipation in her seat. Could her lips spread any wider?

Lennon drops me on the couch and heads over to her purse, grabbing out a white piece of paper.

I try to ignore the niggling inside of me that tells me a lot of what Lennon says is on point, but it's becoming harder and harder.

"Whit?" I whisper, narrowing my eyes. "Have I really lost myself?"

The crinkling of paper signals that Lennon is approaching.

"No," Whit tries to lie, but her diverted eyes speak the truth.

A printed-out receipt floats into my lap and I pick it up, noticing my chipped manicure. So they do have a point.

"Your gift, courtesy of Whitney and I." My couch cushion rises when Lennon throws herself down next to me.

"Thanks. Did you know that paper is the traditional gift for your first anniversary? I have Chase's gift stashed in the closet. Hey." I stand and run into my bedroom, an idea sparking in my head.

I pull out the plastic bin that contains all the gifts I purchase ahead of time, finding the cufflinks and tie clip as well as the printed lyrics of John Legend's *All of Me* on paper.

"What is that?" Whitney asks, sitting down next to me in my walk-in closet.

I hand her the small black box.

Lennon plops on my bed in front of us, blowing out a long breath of air. "Did you buy him a stamp that says 'I'm an asshole?'" She slides down the edge of my bed and crawls over until she's between Whitney and me.

Whitney slowly opens it, and then her eyes veer to me, handing the box to Lennon.

"Oh, Tahl. You were way too good for him." She reaches over, putting her arms around me in a tight hug.

The slamming of the box echoes in my room, and Lennon springs up to her feet. "What else do you have?" she asks, searching my room.

"What?" I ask, standing up.

"Of him. What are you hiding? We had that bonfire a month after and you failed to give us this. I know you're hiding something else." She opens drawers, rifling through all my stuff, and I follow her around closing them and re-organizing them as fast as she's tearing them apart.

"I have nothing. I forgot I even bought those. Take them, I don't care. I'm over Chase Webber." My voice rises the more she circles like an F-5 tornado in my room.

She slides her thin body under my bed. "Do you have a box under here filled with letters or some shit? Though Chase doesn't scream 'sentimental guy.' He couldn't even give you a decent orgasm, for Christ's sake." She comes out the other side and Whitney is there waiting for her, arms crossed over her chest.

"Enough, Lennon," she says, but Lennon throws her hands up in the air.

"You know what? Give me the shirt." She makes a beeline right for me, and I jump on the bed to escape her.

"Len," Whitney says, half laughing, half trying to be the sensible one.

"I hate seeing you like this. I want my anal-retentive friend back. The one who put her spoon in the dishwasher. The boss babe who handled her shit. The one who wore laundered clothes!" She hops on the bed, and I pick up a pillow, throwing it at her.

She hits me in the face with it. Hard.

"Give it up, Tahl."

"You want my shirt? Fine!" I strip off the dirty Stanford t-shirt that I stole from Chase the first time I ever slept over at his condo. A small part of my heart shrivels up and dies as I hand her the final remnant of my life with him.

"Thank you." She tosses the shirt over her shoulder, and it falls at Whitney's cute ankle boots. "Put it in the bag, Whit," Lennon orders, her eyes still square on me.

"Bag?" I ask.

"Don't forget the cufflinks." Lennon ignores my question and Whitney snatches the black box up and then pinches my t-shirt with her thumb and forefinger, carrying it out of the room.

Unable to continue the fight, I fall to my mattress and Lennon falls right next to me.

"I'm sorry, but you need some tough love." Her voice is soft now.

I glance over at her, and there's a small smile on her face. My friends are everything to me, but I've never been the one who needed help. I'm the one who has the high-profile job, the one who exercises six days a week. I have a savings account with some actual money in it, a 401K, an apartment in the heart of the city. We all have a role in our circle of friends and mine is to be the organized one who has her life documented in planners and her shit together.

"I don't remember signing up for the military," I joke, starting to appreciate the friends I have.

"You gotta get out of the funk," Lennon says.

"Literally," Whitney says, the mattress dipping with her addition on the other side of me.

The three of us lie on the bed shoulder to shoulder like sardines. "When did I become so pathetic?" My voice cracks and each of them grab hold of one hand, squeezing tight.

"I would say when your braces cut Jimmy Twendle's lips

when you played seven minutes in heaven in the closet?" Whit jokes and we all laugh.

This is so not me. I'm not one to wallow in my self-pity. I start shimmying Chase's old sweatpants off my body, leaving me in my panties and bra. Thankfully, I haven't lost my matching undergarments obsession.

"Um, I get that it's been six months, but use the vibrator I gave you. I'm over my experimentation phase," Lennon says and scoots away from me. "And for the love of God have your legs waxed."

I roll my eyes. "Put these in the bag." I toss them to her, and she smiles.

"There's our Tahl," Whit says.

We all sit up on my bed. "Great, we're going out," Lennon adds.

"Yeah, we are," I say, rushing over to my closet.

"Let's go dancing," Lennon says, meeting me and flipping through my hangers.

"Can Cole meet us?" Whitney asks and Lennon sighs.

"Cole can stay home." She eyes me and pretends she's annoyed, but we all love Cole.

"I'm going to call him," Whitney says and leaves the room, ignoring Lennon.

She walks in five minutes later, biting her lip.

"Um, are you guys up for something a little different?" Whitney leans her shoulder on the doorframe. I've known Whitney since grade school, and she's worried whatever she has to ask, we're not going to like.

"I thrive on different," Lennon says. "Hey, does Cole have connections into the Regent Bar? Because I'm dying to go there."

"No." She shakes her head. "Just trust me. I think this is exactly what Tahlia needs." She bites her lower lip as her mouth forms a smile. Then she spins on her heels and walks back into my family room.

Lennon and I share a look. My stomach rumbles with uneasiness wondering what 'different' might mean, while Lennon grins like she can't wait to find out.

THE TAXI STOPS ON the side of the street outside San Francisco, and I peer out the window to a huge parking lot with a giant tent set up in the middle, bodies spilling out every open side. What appears to be a rented fence surrounds the parking lot and further back I think I spy a building of some sort.

"What is this?" I ask as Whitney pays the taxi driver, opening her door to exit.

"Excitement, that's what." Lennon hip-checks me until I start sliding out and when we're both finally standing on the pavement, she shuts the door to the taxi and it speeds off.

Whitney pulls out her phone and starts texting Cole, I presume.

Lennon bolts toward the excitement as a kid to a carnival. Whit and I follow and soon Whit tucks her phone in her back pocket.

"Cole's waiting at the gate for us," she says, without any explanation of where we are.

"What is this?" I ask, glancing down at my Capri pants and sandals. I'm not sure what I'm wearing is appropriate.

"It's an amateur boxing fight night. Cole comes here with his friends on occasion." She finally answers my question, and I wish she hadn't.

My throat dries and she must notice my reaction.

"Not Chase." She swings her arm around my shoulders, pulling me into her small frame. "Cole understands that Chase is never to be around me."

I curl further into my friend's security. "What about when you get married?"

She draws back so I can see how serious she is. "We'll elope, or forget to mail his invitation. Cole still has to propose, anyway. First things first."

"It's his brother." A recurring nightmare I've had is that if my best friend marries Chase's brother, I'll have to continually see him at their wedding, their baby showers, their kid's graduation . . .

"Tahl." She waits for me to give her my full attention. Once my eyes are on hers she continues, "Let's not talk about Chase for one night."

"Deal," I say. She unhooks her arm from around my shoulders and we try to catch up with Lennon as masses of people file in front of us.

"This is that hot of a thing?" I ask, noticing it's five guys to one girl waiting to get in.

Lennon moseys back our way. "Shit, what a sausage fest." She elbows me, thinking whenever sausage comes up in conversation she needs to point it out to me since my dad owns the biggest sausage company in North America.

I nod, my eyes floating to the top of my eyelids. It's easier to let the jokes go than to argue.

"There are a lot of guys. I guess Cole had the right idea." Whit and Lennon exchange a look and then glance at me. "You're a shoe-in for a rebound tonight." Whit elbows me.

As I reach to rub the side of my ribs, it all makes sense. Whit also thinks I need to get over Chase by being with another guy. It's not just crazy Lennon—the sensible one in our group, Whit, agrees.

Lennon quickly cozies up to two guys with tattoos covering every inch of visible skin, including their neck. The two of them sandwich her between them and their eyes shine to one another with intrigue.

"WHIT!" a male voice screams, and both of us rise to our tiptoes to peer over everyone.

"Cole," Whitney says, his name dripping with love as she falls to her heels, grabs my hand and starts walking us toward the gate.

"Maybe I'll see you inside, boys," Lennon flirts as I grab her hand and tug her forward.

We walk like we're in grade school, linked like a chain. Upon our approach, Cole hands cash to the guy at the entrance.

"Enjoy the fights," the guy says, giving the three of us a once-over.

"This one," Cole says and picks up Whit, lifting her over the waist-height metal fence, "is taken, but they"—he points to Lennon and me—"are available."

The guy nods his head and stamps our hands, his gaze never leaving us.

I smile politely and step on the metal fence. When I find myself stuck with one leg over the other side, Cole helps me the rest of the way over.

"Hey, Tahl," he says, and I smile. Ever since the wedding fiasco, Cole's face always bears sympathy when he looks at me.

If everything had gone right, Cole would be my brother-in-law, but sadly, his brother doesn't believe in monogamy.

"Hey, Cole. Come here often?" I ask coyly, and he laughs.

"Lennon and Whit giving you pointers in the car?" He eyes

Whit and that humor I had fades.

Cole's in on this too?

As Cole busies to get Lennon to stop flirting with the guy at the door and actually enter whatever this makeshift underground fighting thing is, I look around.

There are six rings staggered under a series of tents. I didn't notice how far back the event goes from the taxi. It's mostly guys walking around with Solo cups, and the smell of cigarettes lingers in the air.

I plug my nose and wave my hand over my face when a guy blows out a stream of smoke as he walks by me.

"Disgusting." I stick my tongue out, and Whit agrees.

Once Cole and Lennon join us, he grabs Whit's hand and we all link together, follow-the-leader style, pushing through the crowd. Cole stops us at a table by the bar area.

Three guys who look like they should be on a commercial for male-pattern baldness sit around the table. One with no hair, one with some, and one with the most.

Lucky for me, I don't recognize them as being anyone I'd ever met through Chase. That's the thing with Cole, though, he hangs out with people not associated with his prestigious surname. Unlike his brother, who always used his name for clout and benefits, Cole's almost embarrassed and tries to keep who his father is a secret.

Cole sits down and pats his lap for Whit, since there are only two open chairs. Not like Whit minds. I've heard enough snippets of their sex life that she's probably grinding on his already-hard dick right now.

I sit while Lennon doesn't.

"Grab me a beer, Tahl, I'll be back." She walks over to the nearest fighting ring, and I soon hear her cheering on red short guy. Literally, she's saying, "Go, red short guy! Make him work for it!"

"She'd fit in anywhere," I comment.

"Not the country club," Whit jokes, because when we were in high school, I took Lennon to my parents' country club and it was the first time I've ever seen her shut her mouth. Not a word the entire event until we left.

"True."

We share a smile, and I'm reminded what great friends I have.

"Okay, this is Tahlia." Cole points over to me as he starts the introductions. His other hand stays firmly planted on his girlfriend's ass. "Tahl, this is Derek, Sammie, and Todd." He points to the three men who look oddly alike.

"Hey," they each say and wave.

"Are you brothers?" I ask, and they look at each other as though they don't know the answer.

"Yeah," Sammie says.

"Nice." I cross my legs and we all chit-chat for a bit before I glance at the bar. "I think I'm going to grab our drinks."

"I'll get them." Cole taps Whitney's ass to move, and she's squirming to stand when I hold my hand up in the air.

"No, I'm good." I position my purse crossways over my body and straighten my shoulders as I walk toward the bar.

The line is moving, and it's like Main Street in a small town with how many people are approaching others and asking them how they're doing. I'm so enamored by the friendliness of this group, a group I'd usually have no contact with, that I don't notice when a guy approaches me.

"Hey, want in?" he asks.

I glance behind me. He's a smaller guy, with dark slicked-back hair and an unkempt beard.

"I'm sorry, what?" I ask, pushing the strands of my blonde hair behind my ear.

"The fight. The final one starts in about . . ." He glances at his Rolex watch. The guy must do well unless it's a fake, but from the quick look I got, it's not. I should know the difference, Chase owned two. "A half hour." I notice a wad of cash in his pocket.

"I'm sorry. This is my first time here. I don't know the fighters."

His eyes zoom over my right shoulder and then back my way, a smile now teasing at his lips. "Want to meet one?" he asks, and instinctively I look to my right and left, waiting to see some guy with red or blue boxer shorts on, but there's no one.

"You going to give me a backstage pass or something?" I ask.

He laughs, revealing a mouth full of capped teeth. "No, babe, I'm not. Listen, these are the rules. It's Brock Hayes and Lucas Cummings tonight. This fight's been expected for some time, and you have a fifty-fifty shot with either one."

Is this guy serious? He expects me just to bet on two guys when I have no idea who they are?

The line moves forward, but every step I take, this guy matches.

"What's your name?" I ask the little gnat who doesn't seem to want to leave me alone.

"Shawn," he answers.

"Okay, Shawn. Here's twenty." I pull the bill from my wallet, discreetly covering my other cash.

"Who you betting on?" he asks, grabbing a raffle ticket and poising his pen, waiting for my reply.

"Um . . ." In my head I'm doing eenie, meenie, miney, mo.

"I'd go for Brock," a guy who's suddenly appeared next to me chimes in.

He has the most gorgeous green eyes. Seriously, like two emeralds lit up with a spotlight. My gaze moves down to his chiseled, scruffy jaw and pouty lips. My stomach flutters, my heartbeat stammers, and heat builds between my thighs.

Who is this man?

"Why?" I ask, swallowing down the saliva pooling in my mouth.

"Lucas is a newbie, and he's the underdog." He widens his stance, crossing his arms over his chest. He's wearing black track pants and a t-shirt that's faded as though it's seen the inside of a washing machine a million times.

"But Shawn says it's a pretty even fight," I argue and the guy looks at Shawn and then back to me.

"He's trying to take your money. Believe me, bet on Brock." He nods and a girl comes over, handing him a water bottle.

"Thanks." She tiptoes up and kisses his cheek. "Tonight?" she asks and I understand her presumption.

Excuse me while I swallow back the bile rising up my throat. Of course, the gorgeous guy is a man whore.

"Thanks for the water," he says and ignores her question. She scurries away and his eyes focus back on me.

Wanting to get these drinks and get back to my table, I dig into my wallet and grab a hundred-dollar bill. "Fine. One hundred on Lucas." I hand my money to Shawn, and he scribbles something on my ticket, handing it over to me.

"If Lucas should win"—he laughs like it's impossible—"come see me over there after it's over for your payout." He points to a long table just past the makeshift bar we're standing in front of, and I nod.

"Sure thing."

The line moves forward, as does Shawn to the people behind me, but the hot guy is still right next to me.

"You like the underdogs?" he asks, taking a sip of his water. I fixate on the way he's licking his lips. Damn, I bet he's one of those awesome kissers. Not that I've ever had a kiss that made my knees weak, but I bet this guy can do it.

"I do." The line disperses and I step up to the bar, ordering a pitcher of beer for the table and a glass of Moscato for myself.

"Sorry. Beer, water, and wine coolers only," the bartender says. I stare blankly at him.

"Vodka?" I ask.

He shakes his head. "Did I say vodka?" he snarls.

"Well, no."

"Come on," the guy behind me whines, and the hot guy shoots him a look that has him taking a step back.

"Give her my stuff, Ted," Muscles says.

The bartender nods and moves into a cooler, grabbing a bottle of Grey Goose vodka. He pours it into a Solo cup and slides it my way.

"I don't suppose you have a lime?" I ask and the gruff silver-haired bartender stares at me with no expression on his face. He screws the top on the vodka and places it back in the cooler.

Hot guy tugs my elbow and we slide to the opposite edge of the bar.

"This isn't exactly your type of place, huh?" he asks, taking another sip of his water.

"Why do you say that?" I ask, a little offended.

A cocky grin reveals a mouth of perfectly white teeth. "Because you look like you're about one second from crying your eyes out."

"No." I inhale a breath. Who is this guy?

I'm here.

I'm dressed.

I'm drinking.

I just bet on a fight.

I'm enjoying myself just fine.

"Maybe I've never been here before, but I'm not upset, nor do I want to cry." I grab the pitcher of beer and my straight vodka.

He cups my elbow to stop me. "I'm sorry. I wasn't trying to offend you. I just wondered why you're here?"

My shoulders fall. "My friends." I point to the table where Whit's tongue is halfway down Cole's throat and two girls are flirting away with the brothers. Lennon is nowhere to be found.

"You're friends with the Mendles?"

I shrug.

"The Mendle brothers. They're the ones who own the gym and host the boxing nights."

"Really?" I ask, looking back over to see their jeans-and-t-shirt-clad bodies. They own a boxing ring? "They're friends with the guy who's being resuscitated by my friend's tongue."

He laughs, and our eyes lock for a beat longer than they should. "Do you give CPR like your friend over there?" He steps closer, and I don't draw back. Maybe this guy isn't as bad as I thought.

"Not on the first meeting, no."

"First date?" he asks, the mint from his gum igniting my awareness.

"I'm not looking for a date right now," I say.

"You're not? How about a new friend?" He picks up my vodka glass and brings it to his lips. He peers at me over the rim of the glass.

"I have a lot of friends."

"No one can ever have enough friends. Plus, I come with great benefits." He tips the cup, and I lose sight of his eyes briefly until he swallows and places the cup down on the bar. I glance to the side to see he's at least left me some of my drink.

"What kind of benefits?" I ask, leaning into him more and wanting him to tell me everything he'd do to me.

"Intrigued?" he asks.

As embarrassed, as I am to admit it, I nod. That arrogant smirk widens. Maybe a rebound screw is what I need, and if I'm going to, I want this guy. This guy can give me what I need—a crazy sex fest where I can't walk for days.

He glances behind us into the crowd and back my way, grabbing his bottle of water from the edge.

"How about you meet me after the fight, and I'll show you the benefits I'll bring to our budding friendship?"

The heat that was building ignites into a wildfire between my legs. I nod, unable to verbally convey my agreement.

"There's a spot on the north side of the tent. Meet me there about a half hour after."

I nod, and he leans in close, his breath tickling my skin.

"I'll need your verbal commitment before I bestow you with my benefits."

Then he backs away, winks one of his emerald eyes and turns on his heel.

Holy shit, did I just agree to a one-night stand?

I PLACE THE PITCHER of beer on the table, and one of the brothers starts pouring. You'd think since they're the hosts tonight, they'd be buying me drinks. It'd be the gentlemanly thing to do. Though Chase never went to the bar without getting me one. So maybe that's not a good sign about being a gentleman. I'll get my own drinks from now on.

The one brother, Sammie, aka 'some hair,' tries to make conversation, asking me about my purse. Seriously, is that what *Cosmo* is telling men to talk about these days to get a woman interested? Get her talking about her accessories? No, thanks. Whit isn't much of a distraction. She's still on Cole's lap even though there's an open chair now. They're in their new relationship bubble, and it's about as annoying as the hangnail I'm picking at. I glance down at my chipped, plum nail polish, already calendaring a manicure for tomorrow.

Lennon skips over to the table, beaming with mischief. The chaos of our surroundings only pulls out more of her quirky personality.

She falls into the chair next to mine. "I just made out with a guy," she whispers like we're thirteen and Jimmy Twendle just flirted with her.

"Great." I take a sip of my drink, letting the burn numb me. Hopefully.

"I heard this next fight is going to rock. The Brock guy is some huge son of a bitch who hasn't lost a fight yet."

She continues to ramble on about his previous fights, so my eyes drift to the crowd, searching for my fellow vodka lover. Sadly, there are too many people to spot him.

"Let's go." Lennon stands, grabs my arm and pulls me forward right to the bar line.

"I already have my drink." I raise my Solo cup, and she rolls her eyes.

"Tonight is the night for you to let loose and alcohol is the only thing that brings out the less anal part of your personality. Speaking of . . . have you ever done anal?"

My eyes widen for a second. "Have you?"

"Um, yeah. Of course. You know that saying? 'Once you go anal you know it's not shameful.'" Her expression says 'duh.'

"I've never heard that saying," I deadpan and move into line with her.

Lennon shrugs. "What is that?" she asks, tiptoeing to look into my glass. "How did you score the hard stuff?" she asks.

"A guy." I shrug.

"A guy," she mimics, waiting for more information.

I look around to make sure there aren't any ears too close. "I met a guy at the bar, and he wants me to meet him after," I say in a low voice so that no one will overhear. But it's useless because she squeals so high every person in a ten-foot radius stops and stares. Lennon's ability to not give a shit shows when she screams even louder the second time.

"About fucking time. You're going to get laid tonight."

My face warms and I change my stance, wishing a

mini-sinkhole would swallow me up.

"Shut up," I bite out, and she rolls those gray eyes of hers.

The line moves, and it's like déjà vu all over again as I inch forward.

"Shut up? You're slutting up, and I love it. Where is he?" She's searching as though the crowd is going to part and he'll appear through the mist.

"I don't know. He said after." I down another gulp of my drink. The thought of a one-night stand almost makes me itch from hives.

"Awesome. And from the looks of things around here, any one of these guys can probably give you multiple orgasms." My mouth hangs open, and she eventually looks over. "Come on, Tahl. I know Chase was a selfish lover."

I bite back a response that would protect Chase, but the truth is, he never really seduced me. Half the time, I brought myself to completion in the bathroom afterward. Heck, probably ninety percent of the time. I really need to stop giving him the benefit of the doubt.

I shrug, not in the mood to talk about my ex-fiancé, since I still feel like I must not have been that great of a lover to him since he was getting laid all over the place while we were engaged. There's nothing worse for the ego.

Thinking about Chase, I down the remaining vodka and hold the cup in my hand.

Our turn comes, and Lennon leans over the edge of the bar.

"Okay, Ted."

She knows his name?

"What do you have? You're hiding the good stuff some-where." She takes out a hundred-dollar bill and waves it in front of his face. "What will it take?"

Ted, the burly bartender from earlier, smiles and he has an almost friendly appearance now with his lips curled upward.

"Lennon," he sighs. Then he turns around and moves aside two coolers.

"Please tell me how you're on a first-name basis with the bartender when we've been here for like an hour?"

She flutters her eyelashes. "I'm friendly."

I let it go, and Ted comes back over with a bottle of Everclear.

"No way, Lennon." I shake my head, getting Ted's attention.

"Two, please," Lennon says, tucking the hundred-dollar bill in his front pocket and then patting him on the cheek.

"I'm not drinking it," I tell her, but in usual Lennon fashion, she ignores any arguments that aren't in agreement with her.

"Have a nice night, ladies." Ted smiles again, and I'm thrown once again by his attitude adjustment.

"See you in a bit, Ted," Lennon says and grabs the empty cup from my hand, dropping it in a nearby trashcan. Then she hands me the hundred-and-eighty-proof drink.

I'm not a huge drinker, and I've seen my friends wasted on Everclear more than once. One time back in college I stopped Lennon from stripping at a frat party. Another time Whit thought a keg of beer was her boyfriend and started French-kissing the barrel. How many times have I paid taxi cleaning bills from Chase's destructive behavior after drinking Everclear? It sucks, and I'm not about to become its next victim.

"I said no, Lennon." I shake my head, refusing to take the drink from her hands, but she urges me so I finally relent just to shut her up.

"You're going to have a one-night stand sober?" She cocks her head. "Not a good idea."

I roll my eyes, and Lennon doesn't stop at the table. Rather, she leads me toward the front of the ring.

Whit jumps off Cole's lap, and he grabs her wrist before she can get away too fast.

"Are you sure your lips can handle the break?" I joke, and she distorts her face into a 'you think you're funny' expression.

Cole finishes his sentence to the brothers and then stands, saying his goodbyes, and the two of them join us.

"This is exciting," Whit says as we're standing in the first row by the ring, thanks to Lennon's complete disregard for anyone around her.

"Exciting? This is fucking awesome," Lennon says. "How did you keep this from us, Cole?" She's bouncing on her toes as though she's two seconds away from crawling under the ropes and swinging fists herself.

"Calm down, girl." I eye her and then Whit and I each shake our heads at our best friend.

"I'm trying to work something out with the brothers, so I only found out about it recently," Cole admits, bringing Whitney in front of him and wrapping his arms around her middle.

Oh, how I long for that affection again.

I down a gulp of Everclear. Lennon puts her arm around my neck and pours some of her drink into mine.

"Lennon! No."

"Shh . . . you need it more than me," she whispers in my ear and then the music stops and bodies push against my back.

"Oh, it's starting," Whitney coos and Lennon releases me only to start jumping up and down like we're in the middle of a mosh pit.

She doesn't know these men, so I have no idea why she's so invested.

Sammie weaves through the ropes with a microphone in his hand. He looks down at us and winks and then greets the crowd.

"Boy, do we have a treat for you tonight. Brock Hayes and Lucas Cummings are our final fight. Let's do introductions first." He pauses, and the sea of people parts as a guy with a black hooded silk robe concealing his body walks toward the ring with two guys on each side.

"Did we just step into Caesars? Seriously, he needs body-guards?" I remark and Whitney pushes my shoulder, urging me to live a little and not dissect every minute detail.

The guy jumps up on the ring, weaving his body through the ropes. His back is to me as he shifts his weight between each foot.

"Gentleman and the few ladies," Sammie says, winking to me once again. "Lucas 'The Raging Bull' Cummings!"

The boxer pushes his hood off his head, stepping into the middle of the ring with his gloved fist up in the air.

"Holy shit," I say, and Lennon turns my way. "That's him." My stomach clenches and heat flares in my cheeks.

"Your one-night stand?" Lennon steps back to my side to hear me over the cheering crowd.

"Yeah."

My mouth waters as the guy who propositioned me a half hour ago strips off his robe, revealing a set of abs I'm quite positive could wash the panties I just soaked. Jesus, he's hot, with not one ounce of fat on him. His black silk shorts have a white band of fabric around his waist that says Raging Bull.

Lennon grabs my cup out of my hand.

"Hey," I say, reaching for it.

"No, girl, you're gonna want to be stone sober for this one. You don't want to be like Whit the first night she and Cole got together." She takes a sip, but I grab the cup back, knowing I need it more than I thought.

Especially when he glances down and a perfect set of sparkling teeth emerge, revealing a smile that has me gripping Lennon's arm for support. Then he bites his bottom lip for a second, and my fingernails dig into Lennon's bicep.

"Damn, I wish I saw him first." Lennon's voice sounds as dreamy as I feel. "You better ride him like you're a fucking rodeo star, girl." And there's the Lennon I know and love.

The vodka man, now known as Lucas Cummings, turns around, continuing to bounce on his toes.

Sammie's voice rings out once more, and another boxer enters with four bodyguards and a red silk robe. He weaves through the ropes and stares down Lucas. Lucas laughs, egging him on, and my gut twists.

"The undefeated Brock 'Lights Out' Hayes," Sammie announces, and the guy jumps around the ring, waving both fists in the air.

Lucas turns back toward us, but his attention is focused solely on another guy. A small man rushes in the ring, putting Vaseline on his cheeks and forehead.

"This is the real deal." The excitement in Lennon's voice increases.

Lucas keeps peeking over at me, an uptick on his lips each time. Eventually, the guy who I assume is his manager glances over our way to see what's distracting him.

Whit tugs on my arm and leans in close. "Someone has caught the boxer's attention," she whispers and I wish my cheeks didn't heat like they are.

"Because he's thinking of all the ways he's going to fuck her later," Lennon adds, turning her head for only a second.

"What?" Whitney asks, in the dark on the whole situation.

"I met him at the bar. He asked me to meet him after," I say, and Whitney's eyes crinkle as if she doesn't think that's a good idea. So thinks the girl who resorted to Tinder.

"Like you'd do that," she says confidently, and I bite my lower lip. The lip that is now a little tingly from what I assume is the Everclear. "Tahlia, don't you think you should wait for your second one-night stand for someone of his . . . caliber?"

Cole peeks over her shoulder. "I met him a few weeks ago when I came to watch the fights. Seems like an okay guy."

Whitney raises her hand, and it smacks Cole in the face.

He grabs his nose.

"Oh, I'm sorry." She glances at him for a second before her eyes set on me again like a mother scolding her teenager.

"No, babe, it's my fault. I know better than to try to get in the middle of a conversation between you three." Cole touches his nose a few times and wiggles it around.

"Guess you're not the kinda guy to jump in that ring then." Lennon laughs and points at him. Cole raises his eyebrows in her direction.

"Are you challenging me, Lennon?" Cole asks and the three of us laugh.

Whitney waves her hands around. "Forget that. Tahlia, you can't go have a one-night stand with someone like him."

I look past Whitney to Cole. "I think you need to go over the one-night stand rules. First one being, you don't know the person. Second qualification, you pick the hottest guy."

Cole laughs, but Whitney only becomes more agitated. I'm not sure why she's giving me trouble. She's the one who brought me here tonight.

"Tahl," she sighs.

"Whit," I mimic her tone. "I'm a grown woman. I'll be fine."

Lennon elbows me a few times. "The blood is about to spew," she says and jumps up, screaming, "Go, black shorts!"

Lucas turns around to Lennon and then cocks an eyebrow in her direction. For a second, jealousy spikes within me, but when his gaze turns to me and he smirks, I melt. Unable to deal with the thought that the guy up in the ring could be inside of me in a few hours, I tip the rest of my Everclear and down it.

chapter

FOUR

THE FIGHT IS OVER before I even get a second to appreciate the barbaric concept of beating the shit out of another human being. Blood smears the floor of the ring, but that's nothing compared to the cut above Lucas's eye or the redness over his entire body. Why would anyone want to do this?

"Your boy won!" Lennon raises my hand like I have some sort of investment in his win.

Oh, wait, I do. He was the underdog, and I bet one hundred dollars on him. Well, I'll be damned.

I tug my arm down, and Lennon is jumping around like an ankle-biting Chihuahua.

Then, out of the blue, with a group of people following him, Lucas slinks under the last rope and I stand there speechless as he approaches me.

"I'm going to run into the shower," he says as I focus on the cut, wondering if my lips will heal it. Girls hover behind him, as do guys, waiting for his attention.

"Okay."

He steps closer, and Lennon backs up while Whitney stands

closer. Lucas's eyes shift toward Whit for a second and he must notice Cole. He extends his hand toward Cole, and I miss his attention already. Seriously, am I this horny?

"Hey. Cole, right?" he asks.

Cole steps forward, shaking his hand. "Yeah, great fight."

"Thanks. Hayes is a son of a bitch, but maybe tonight was his off night."

"Or you're a badass," Lennon chimes in and Lucas' vision shifts to her.

He smiles. "You were my own little cheerleader." He puts his hand out in front of her. "Lucas."

"Lennon." She hip-checks me, and since I have no muscle holding my body up at the moment, I knock into Whit, who falls into Cole, a weight solid enough to hold us. "I'm this one's friend."

Their hands drop and I get Lucas' solo attention again, and my stomach grows giddy. "I hope she has room for one more friend," he says, and a growl comes out of Whitney's mouth while Lennon rears her head back in laughter.

"Let's put it this way, Lucas . . ." Lennon continues overriding the conversation.

Again, his eyes shift to her. "Don't tell me the list is full," he says, with mock indignation.

"She's scratching names off the list for you, buddy," Lennon says, and then a guy walks by, and her eyes follow him like a dog chasing a butterfly. "See you girls later." She raises her hand, and another huff leaves Whitney's mouth.

"I'm sorry, I didn't catch your name," Lucas says, holding his hand out to her.

She stares down at it and back up to him and then back to his hand. Cole nudges her, and she eventually shakes his hand.

"I'm Whitney, her conscience for tonight." She nods her head to the side at me.

I laugh, and his eyes flicker to me. Cole wraps his arms around his girlfriend's shoulders.

"Excuse us, Lucas. My girlfriend needs to remember she's not Tahlia's mother."

The two of them leave even with Whitney's reservations. I swear I can feel her eyes in the back of my head.

"Tahlia, huh?" Lucas asks, and I'm so busy examining the injuries on his beautiful face, I forget he's speaking to me until he touches my shoulder. Like a jolt of electricity, I'm alert.

"I'm sorry, what?" I ask, focusing on his beautiful green eyes staring right back at me.

"Your name, Tahlia, it's beautiful," he says and the way he says my name is so soft and gentle, I'm not as concerned about going home with him.

Then someone knocks into me, pushing me forward, and I knock into him. The sweat still trickling down his chest makes my hands slide down his sculpted abs until the front of my hand grazes the front of his shorts and I'm pretty sure the half-hard thing I just felt is his dick. Unable to step back because of the people wanting to talk to him, I try to remove myself, but I'm locked.

He glances down at me, a cocky smile in place. "All you had to do was ask. I'd never turn down a hand job."

Utter mortification. Blood surges through my body, and I can only imagine that my face resembles Ronald McDonald's nose.

The group behind me and the group behind him are growing impatient, so he grabs my shoulders, shifting me to his side. "Go get something to drink. I'll meet you by Shawn." He winks, and just like that I realize that I forgot all about my bet. "You can collect your winnings and then you can finish that hand job." A playful grin pulls up one side of his mouth.

I have no words, no banter back because I don't do jokes and comebacks. I'm not someone with quick wit who can hammer out jabs or insults right back, so I smile.

"Okay," I say and slide through the masses of people back to my friends.

Lucas gets swallowed up by the crowd, all eager for his attention, and I wonder why all these people want a piece of him.

A half hour later, I'm on my second glass of Everclear with a pocket full of winnings and Whitney's seemed to relax about Lucas. She's so overprotective of me, always handling me with tender hands. But I'm a big girl who's managed to survive this long.

But apparently, this big girl isn't prepared for the way Everclear hits me after I finish consuming it. My lips are past the tingling, my head is past the lightheadedness, and if I could step outside of my body for a moment, I'd see myself dancing in the middle of the bar with Lennon.

I circle around, and two emerald eyes stop me mid-hip swing. Lucas is just sitting there, leaning back in a folding chair, one ankle casually resting on his opposite knee. His cut hand is wrapped around a Solo cup as he brings it up to his lips and takes a slow drink. My eyes fix on his, unable to turn my gaze away. I'm not sure how long I stand there in the middle of Lennon's makeshift circle before she places her two hands on my back and pushes me forward.

Remember when I said Everclear was bad? My foot gets stuck on something, and I pitch forward.

Could I have fallen into Lucas' lap? Possibly.

Could I have given his dick another graze of my hand? I wish.

Instead, I bypass Lucas and catapult onto the table, knocking down every last pitcher and cup. I fail to grab hold of anything as the slickness from the spilled drinks makes my body slide across the table, and I crash into the ground.

The music screeches to a halt, as does the cacophony of people talking. I squeeze my eyes shut. Whitney and Lennon rush to my side, each grabbing an arm to help me up. There's no way I can look into Lucas' eyes at this point, nor can I fathom sleeping with him after this mortification.

They get me to my feet and Cole comes over, looking my body over for any sign of injury.

"I'm fine. Just get me out of here," I whisper-yell.

"It was just a drunken fall. No biggie," Lennon says.

"I told you she couldn't handle Everclear," Whitney snaps at Lennon.

"Stop treating her like she's damaged goods," Lennon snaps back, letting go of my arm.

"Her fiancé was cheating on her! They were together for seven years. She's not the kind of girl who goes out on the prowl drinking and having one-night stands." Whitney's voice rises, and I'm sure everyone in the vicinity can overhear them. I dread looking over at Lucas so I don't.

"Stop talking," Cole shouts over us, trying to be the voice of reason.

"He's your brother. The douche, the asshole!" Lennon baits because she's as drunk as me.

This whole night out was a terrible idea.

"Just because we share blood doesn't mean I agree with what he did. *I* don't condone cheating, Lennon." His voice signifies that she does.

"Everyone stop," I say, my voice low.

"Still, though. Tahl needs to live a little, Whit. She was playing house while he was busy trying to be Hugh Hefner. If she wants to sleep with boxer boy, let her," Lennon yells and I groan, not from the pain in my hip from the fall—because I'm certain a huge bruise will be there tomorrow—but because I glance away from our group to find Lucas intently listening to every word.

"Thanks, girls. Thanks." I unhook my arms from them and stomp away.

"I'm sorry," Whitney says, rushing to my side.

"Me too. We should have kept our mouth shut." Lennon pulls up on my other side.

I remain silent because these two just embarrassed me in front of a drool-worthy guy even more than I already did myself.

"I'll get the car," Cole says, walking past us, and he disappears toward the parking lot.

The three of us stand there, and both of them look me over as though I'm splintered glass about to shatter. The music has picked up again, and people are laughing and having a fun time. Hopefully, too inebriated to remember the girl who face-planted across the table in the morning. God, what if someone had a camera and I end up being the next YouTube sensation?

I groan.

"Tahlia." The softness of Lucas' voice helps to calm my frazzled nerves.

I look up to find his hands tucked into the pockets of his jeans, a duffle bag swung over his shoulder, and his eyes silently begging me to say yes to whatever he's about to ask me.

"Can we talk?" he asks.

Whitney and Lennon both step back, but Cole's Jeep pulls up to the curb.

"We'll be in the car," Whitney says, and they disappear into the vehicle.

He cups my elbow and guides me away from the Jeep toward the fence, then drops his duffle bag to the ground. He places one hand on the fence and leans his weight against it. Unable to relax, I stand there with my arms crossed over my beer-stained blouse.

"You okay?" he asks, tenderness in his tone.

"Yeah." My eyes focus down on the cracked cement.

"I'm guessing tonight isn't a good night?" I can't look at him, so the only way we could sleep together tonight would be if he were to blindfold me. Which wouldn't be a half-bad idea any other time, I suppose.

"No." I figure I'll never see this guy again. I mean, we definitely hang in different circles. My head lifts and I meet his eyes. "I'm sorry. I just got out of a relationship six months ago, and my friends thought I should step out of my normal box."

"The perfect box?" he asks, the sly grin from earlier emerging.

"My friends weren't lying. This isn't my scene." I gesture toward the tent area.

"Would you like it to be?"

My eyes slowly drift to meet his once more. His gaze is seeking. "You have to be over getting to know me already, and you don't even know my last name."

He bellows a laugh. "The only reason I need your last name is to track you down after tonight. That is if you don't give me your phone number."

A rumbling erupts in my stomach. At first, I think it's butterflies fluttering from him still wanting something to do with me, but I quickly realize it's the grumbling of vomit circling in my stomach.

I need to get out of here fast. My eyes search for a trashcan. Nothing.

"You still want my number?" I ask, hiccupping as acid sneaks up my throat.

"Yeah, I kind of like to unwrap perfect boxes. You'd be surprised what I find."

If my throat wasn't burning and my stomach wasn't churning, I'd be swooning. Unable to say anything, I cover my mouth and Lucas' whole persona changes from suave to panic.

I widen my eyes, searching for anything to throw up in. There's not even a tree anywhere in sight. Before I can run past him and throw up in the middle of the sidewalk, the vomit rushes up my throat and I bend over, emptying the contents of my stomach at his feet.

Once I'm at the point of dry-heaving, the tears in my eyes clear enough for me to focus and I realize that I've thrown up in Lucas' duffle bag.

Lennon's suddenly beside me, pulling back my long blonde hair. "Are you okay, sweetie?"

Though my stomach feels much better, I just added another layer of embarrassment to tonight.

Covering my mouth, not to add my horrible breath to the mix, I mumble my apology, but Lucas' eyes fixate on the bag.

"Let me take the bag and I'll get your clothes cleaned. I'll buy you a new one—"

He stops me with his hand. "Unless you know a cleaner that will wash my money, it's useless," he says and Lennon breaks out laughing.

I hit her in the stomach, and she covers her mouth with her hand to stop herself. "This is classic," she says from behind her hand, completely disregarding the seriousness of the situation.

"Lucas," I sigh, ready to bend on my knees to apologize for the umpteenth time, when he puts his hand up in the air.

He looks only at Lennon. "You should get your girl home."

Lennon grabs my arm, dragging me down the sidewalk as I continue to shout apologies. He ignores me as he stares down at his bag, running his hands through the long layers of his honey-blond hair.

Could my life get any worse?

FIVE

"I COME BEARING CAFFEINE." Whitney strolls by me, cheerful and happy with a tray of coffees and a bag that I pray hides bagels because something has to soak up this alcohol.

"Morning, Whit," I mumble, following her down the hall leading to my kitchen.

I sidle up to the breakfast bar, and Whit stands on the other side, placing the coffees on the counter and then searching for a plate.

"Where's Lennon?" she asks, her head buried in my cabinet.

"In my bed." I rest my heavy head in my hand, watching her do what I usually do.

Whit glances over her shoulder and raises her eyebrows.

"She refused to sleep on the couch. Said it would be like old times. I just wanted the night to end, so I stopped arguing."

Whit laughs and pulls out a plate before digging into my cutlery drawer, retrieving a knife. One by one she slices the bagels and my stomach jumps for joy.

"I'm really sorry, Tahl." Her voice is low and sincere. "It

was supposed to be a fun night out." She places the plate in front of me and then opens the variety of cream cheeses she bought, setting them out.

"It was fun. Until it was mortifying," I say, thankful my consumption of Everclear is preventing me from being able to truly envision what a disaster last night was.

The memory of Lucas' eyes as he stared at the bag of money covered with my taco salad from lunch pushes to the forefront of my mind. I push the recollection back as far as it will go, as shivers run up my spine.

Whit circles around the counter and slides into the chair next to me. Her hand lands on my forearm, and when I get the energy to look over, her eyes have more than enough pity in them. "Cole said he's a super-cool guy. He's sure he doesn't hold it against you."

I stare over at her for longer than I should. Mostly because I forgot where my line of thinking was heading.

"Lucas, I'm talking about Lucas," Whitney reminds me as though I'm not the vice-president of the biggest sausage company in North America. Okay, that makes my case worse.

"I'm sure his mind was swimming with thoughts of me as he washed and dried all his money. I mean, I'd do the same thing." I'm sarcastic, and Whit rolls her eyes, focusing all her attention on the bagel with cream cheese.

"It wasn't that bad," she mumbles over her first bite of breakfast.

I take a sip of my coffee, having no energy to fight Operation Throw Bullshit at Tahlia.

We sit there for a few minutes, her loud chewing grating on that last nerve I woke up with while I sip my coffee and contemplate where the biggest rock in San Francisco is so I can crawl under it.

Then the person responsible for my embarrassment saunters

out of my bedroom in her mismatched bra and underwear. The hair on the right side of her head is a mess and pointing up to the sky, but she manages a mischievous smile.

"What's up, hookers?" She grabs some coffee and a bagel and moves over to my couch, making herself comfortable.

"Get off the furniture with that bagel," I mumble, and her head falls over in laughter.

She stands. "Just wondering if the good old Tahlia was still in there." Instead, she hops up on the counter, crossing her legs and staring over at us as though she's waiting for some rundown. "How ya feeling?" she asks me, and I glare back.

"Let's see. Depressed, hopeless, and unattractive. So, that fabulous idea of taking me out last? Top notch." I put my thumb up and shoot her a fake smile. "Oh, and add in nauseated, sore, and did I mention unattractive?"

She waves me off, her face contorting into a look similar to the one I used to give my mother when I was a teenager. "It's like a lasting impression, you know? He'll never forget you."

Her reply earns two thumbs, so I place my coffee down and raise my thumbs in Fonzie's signature move. "Great. Hope I run into him again sometime soon."

"Cole said he fights almost every weekend," Whitney says around a piece of bagel in her mouth.

When I turn her way with a scathing expression, she almost chokes it out from laughing.

"Or not," she says.

Grabbing my coffee, I stand and make my way over to my couch. "Girls, I appreciate the effort, and maybe in time I'll be able to go out again, but not for a while."

"Tahl, everyone has embarrassing moments. Look at Cole and me, that wasn't exactly the best introduction," Whit says.

She may be right, but I'm just not used to making a fool of myself. Everything in my life is meticulously planned. If someone showed me a tape of last night, I probably wouldn't even recognize myself.

"Yeah, let's mourn Tickled Pink." Lennon tips her head down, mock-praying for her first vibrator's untimely death at the jaws of Whitney's dog, Sparky.

"Some people are meant to be the partiers and others are meant to be the ones who take care of the partiers. I'm the latter. I've been the latter my entire life and I'll forever be the latter."

"The hell you will," Lennon says, hopping off the counter. "What did being that way get you? A cheating bastard of a fiancé, that's what. You need to live a little. You need a guy who'll undo that straight jacket you've put yourself in."

"Lennon." Whitney tries to tamp her down, but we both know once she's on a rant there's no stopping her.

"You need to get fucking laid."

There, she's finished, and I can't argue with her. I do need to get laid.

"Well—" I'm about to agree with her when she throws her latest sex toy in my lap.

She announced last fall that she was starting a sex toy company and wanted Whitney and me to try her products. Only Lennon, I swear.

"This one is called Candy Swirl, and it's so much better than Tickled Pink."

She continues on her sales pitch that truthfully I only hear every other word of, but get the gist that this vibrator will do its job and get a girl off.

"Oh." She picks up the piece of paper lying on the table, the one they gave me last night. She holds it up to Whit, and they share a conniving smile. "We never talked about this because you went off on that whole boring paper-anniversary scavenger hunt that led to jackass's name coming into the conversation once again."

I hold out my hand for the piece of paper, but she folds it and holds on to it as she and Whit take a seat in the two chairs across from me.

"So, I know last night was a train wreck, and really, I think we can all blame the Everclear." Whitney starts the pitch, which means they think she'll be able to sell me on whatever they're up to.

"Everclear ruins everything." Lennon purses her lips and shakes her head, as though she wasn't the one practically pouring it down my throat.

I narrow my eyes at her but don't speak.

"We bought you a gift. It's an apology gift because you were blinded by love, but we should've been able to see Chase for the ass he was. We want to make it up to you." She holds her hand out for the piece of paper clenched in Lennon's hands. Lennon passes it to her, and Whitney holds it out between us. "Please, Tahlia, don't refuse it right away, okay?"

I take the paper and unfold it while Whitney and Lennon both fidget in their seats.

I read it over and don't say anything.

It's a one-month subscription to an adventure dating club, called Single In SF. The group goes skydiving, winery-touring, bungee-jumping. Different out-of-the-norm dates that you go on with a group of single people. Interesting and as far out of my comfort zone as it can get.

"I told you," Lennon says. "She'll never do it." Never mind art, I'm pretty sure she majored in manipulation at college. As if I don't know she's trying to use reverse psychology.

"Give it time to absorb." Whitney joins me over on the couch, her hand on my knee. "Tahl, you've always dated one type of guy. The rich guy, the fraternity guy, the daddy's boy. We figured this would get you out there away from guys like that."

"Someone who doesn't think it's a felony if he leaves the

house without gel in his hair. A man who doesn't care if his shirt is wrinkled. Someone who wants to put effort into finding his next girlfriend rather than whoever he picks up at the bar." Lennon stands and then sits across from me on my coffee table so that our knees are practically touching.

I'd normally tell her to get up, but their gift is meaningful and at the same time terrifying. Especially since I'll be doing it alone.

I inhale a large breath. "Okay," I agree.

"Really?" Whit's eyes bug out of her head.

"Pay up." Lennon holds her hand out to Whitney, and she smacks it.

"You guys made a bet?" I ask.

"Actually, we weren't supposed to tell you that." Whitney stares directly at Lennon as though she's a dumbass.

"So neither of you think I can do it?"

"We think you can do it, we just aren't sure you *will* do it. You aren't exactly outdoorsy. I mean, Tahlia, you did that lame indoor track marathon last year," Lennon says.

"Let's make a bet," I tempt them, and Lennon's eyes light up, while Whitney's shoulders deflate. "If I do this dating thing, you guys can't set me up, or drag me out again. Ever."

"What if you're like forty and live with twenty cats?" Whitney asks, and I can't hide my laugh.

"Okay, you can't fix me up or drag me out until I'm surrounded by cat shit."

"You'll never make it," Lennon challenges and holds out her hand.

"We'll see about that."

I hold the paper tighter and stand up before making my way into my kitchen. Grabbing a bagel and smearing it with cream cheese, I take a bite, feeling emboldened now that I have a challenge. I'll show them. Four weeks at an adventure dating club, easy-peasy.

"You tempted the beast," Whitney says, tapping Lennon's shoulder to grab her attention away from the Candy Swirl she's picked up off the couch to examine.

Lennon looks up at me. "That girl can never back away from a challenge."

I know they planned this whole bet thing out. I might feel half dead right now, but Lennon doesn't have loose lips. I'll let them believe they have an advantage because after four weeks and no prospects, I'll be able to do what I want without either of them trying to pull me out of my comfort zone ever again.

You can do anything for four weeks, right?

SIX

I'M NOT SURE WHAT I expected when I signed up for the horseback riding adventure with Single In SF, but I didn't expect to be squeezing between Range Rovers and Mercedes to park. Shouldn't there be rows of rusty old pickups around? I mean, I'm stepping on hay as I climb out of my car. Surely the Mercedes didn't haul it over. The only car that doesn't cost more than eighty grand around here is some rundown truck that looks like the top has been sawed off.

My riding boots squish under the mud below the layer of hay from last night's rainfall, and I tuck my cell phone and keys into the pocket of my sweatshirt. Not sure whose bright idea it was to plan an outdoor activity when the warm summer weather hasn't arrived in San Francisco yet. It's still spring, and the temperature is in the mid-fifties.

Groups of guys and girls cluster off to the side of a table set up near the entrance. A line has formed in front of the table, and I hear people giving their names, so I step in line.

I glance around to check everyone out, after which I'm fairly certain most of these people are executives like myself.

Their North Face jackets, clean jeans and brand-new boots give them away. Half of them have their faces buried in their cell phones, and the other half are bragging to one another about their jobs. My God, am I one of these types of people? Is this how I come across to someone who doesn't know me? I cringe inwardly at the thought.

The line moves and I step forward. A few of the guys on the periphery shift their eyes away from the girls they're talking to.

Is this how these things work? Is this going to be like when the new girl starts school and all the guys flock to her until the next new girl comes? I'm the shiny new iPhone to this group of Adventure Daters.

One guy's eyes zoom in on me, and I turn quickly, pulling my phone out to distract myself. I'm thumbing through Facebook posts of what happy people do on their weekends while I wait to horseback-ride with strangers.

"Hi." His voice is squeaky as though he's going through puberty, but his full-growth beard says he's much older than that.

I glance over from my phone for a second. "Hey," I say, burying my head back into the abyss of Facebook. Man, some of these people have amazingly happy lives according to their posts.

"You're new?" he asks, and I glance over again.

"Yeah. First day."

He's kind of cute, a tad shorter than I prefer, but lean muscle and from the glimpse at the watch adorning his wrist, I know he has money. Upon further inspection, I notice a collared button-up shirt under his North Face fleece. His perfectly white teeth sparkle under the sunlight, and I realize he's Chase.

Not the actual Chase, but his replica. As I look around the area, each guy has perfectly coifed hair, shaped eyebrows, shirts tucked in, pants not too short or too long as though tailor-made for their specific size. Add in the cars in the parking lot, and these are all the type of guys I'd once been attracted to.

I chuckle to myself. Whit and Lennon thought this would expose me to someone outside of my norm when all it did was thrust me into the snake pit with all of them.

"Is something funny?" Chase's mini-doppelgänger says.

"Oh." I stop laughing at the absurdity of my life. "No. I'm sorry." I hold out my hand to him. "I'm Tahlia."

His smile emerges again. "Tahlia, what a beautiful name. I'm Aaron." He shakes my hand in a wimpy fashion as though he's afraid my bones will crack.

Whatever, dude. I just lifted half my weight at the gym this morning.

"Hi, Aaron." I snatch my hand back when he tries to hold on a little too long and palm my phone again.

"I'm a vice-president at Godfrey's Bank. Youngest ever promoted."

My eyes lift from my phone, and I smile with a nod. "Congratulations."

"What do you do?" he asks, stepping ahead with me as the line moves forward.

"I'm a . . ." I stall because I'm not sure I want these people to be able to track me down after today is through. Aaron's eager smile screams stalker to me. "A Pilates instructor."

His eyes roam down my body, and I almost follow his vision, second-guessing my claim, but I shove my phone in my pocket and straighten my back. I work hard for my body. Six days at the gym every week. Even after Chase left I never missed a day.

"I can tell."

A genuine smile parts my lips. It's nice to know I'm still attractive. "Thanks." My smile must be a little too inviting because he steps closer at the same time the line in front of me clears and a pair of green emeralds sparkling with amusement lock onto mine.

Eyes so familiar my thighs squeeze together.

"You?" I say, my voice too breathless.

"You?" he mimics my tone, raising eyebrows that are way too perfectly shaped not to be waxed or threaded.

Lucas is seated behind the table and looks down at his clipboard for a second, his eyes scrolling until he looks back up to me.

"You're here to find a date?" That pen in his hand puts a checkmark next to my name. "Tahlia Santora?"

I nod, my voice locked with one-inch chains.

"As in the Santora Sausage company?" Aaron asks next to me, and my eyes flicker over to him. I'd forgotten all about him.

I begin to nod before I shake my head back and forth. "No, but I still get the lame jokes about how I like my sausages." I tighten my smile, hoping they each buy it.

Lucas's smile widens, revealing more perfect, white teeth.

Aaron laughs. "You must have been razzed about that your whole life."

I stare blankly at him, but he continues laughing.

"Hey, Aaron. Since Tahlia's new, let me get her signed in, and then you can stake your claim," Lucas says.

Aaron stops laughing, placing all his attention on Lucas. The smile doesn't reach the edge of his lips, let alone his eyes, but he nods. "Yeah, hands off, Cummings," he threatens.

Lucas doesn't respond and waits for Aaron to step far enough away before he speaks again.

"How are you?" he whispers, so I lean in closer to the table.

"I'm fine," I whisper back.

The oddest thing about this situation is that the embarrassment of seeing him again lasted all of two seconds. There's a comfort with Lucas I've never experienced with anyone else.

He chuckles and then looks over my shoulder.

"Why don't you slide over here and I'll check these people in before we get your papers signed." He points to a barrel behind the folding table he's seated at.

I slide around him and take a seat on the barrel as Lucas makes quick work of the line. He knows most of the people, and he quickly checks them off the list. The girls hover a little longer, and I can feel the men's eyes on me while Lucas is helping them.

After the group is checked in and they mingle with their steaming cups of Starbucks coffee, Lucas's attention turns to me.

"Okay, so since you have the lucky little red star next to your name, I need you to fill out these papers and sign the release form." He hands me the clipboard with the papers.

I look them over and sign, releasing all rights to sue the company should I get injured. When I finish, I pass the clipboard back to him.

He studies the papers, making sure everything is a go.

"I'm sorry for the other night," I say quietly, so only he can hear.

He glances at me from the corner of his eye, smirks and then turns his attention back to the papers.

"No problem." He shrugs. "It's not like I've never been shitfaced before."

"Yeah, but your money . . ."

He nods, his lips pursing. "Didn't make for the best night, but it didn't devalue it, so we're square."

He stands, and I follow suit while he places the pen back in the holder on the clipboard, holding it down at his hip.

"Lucas," I sigh, but he shakes his head.

"Apology accepted." His voice says he's done hearing any more about it, so I nod, accepting that fact.

"Okay. Thank you."

The smile he gives me reminds me of the first night I met him. So carefree and easy-going.

"Now, what are you doing adventure dating?" he asks, a crease forming on his forehead.

"My friends dared me that I wouldn't do it." I shrug.

He begins sauntering toward the rest of the people here and I fall into step with him.

"You do know that if your friends dare you to jump off the Transamerica Pyramid Building, you shouldn't do it, right?" He raises his eyebrows, and I giggle like I'm a fifteen-year-old girl.

"I'm not that dumb, but it was a gift, and I know they think I'll last one outing and call it quits, but I'm no quitter."

He stops me with a hand on my elbow right before we're within earshot of the others. His brief touch sends a cascade of goosebumps up my arm. "I'm glad this won't be the only time I see you. Welcome." He smiles, and we lock stares.

"Thank you," I say, heat creeping up my cheeks, and I'm sure I must be blushing.

We stand there for a moment until the annoying gnat I met earlier interrupts us.

"Are we going to get going?" Aaron whines. Lucas' jaw clenches, but he loosens it quick.

"Let's go see a man about a horse." He nods his head toward the others and I follow him up a small hill that leads to a large barn with a paddock beside it. A bunch of different-colored horses are lined up inside the paddock with people who look like they know what they're doing.

I follow Lucas. His jeans hang off his hips perfectly, and I understand a little better what Anastasia Steele was going on and on about every time she saw Christian Grey wear denim. His faded sweatshirt hugs his broad shoulders, and I imagine my hands searching for the body I saw the other night under the layers of warmth. The way he wears his baseball cap backward makes him appear younger in years. I clench my hands into fists as I reach the rise of the hill because I'm picturing myself flipping off his hat and digging my fingers through the golden hues of his hair.

"Tahlia." His voice pulls me from my daydreaming just as

I imagine his lips on my neck.

I gather myself quickly. I think Lucas just introduced me to the group, so I smile and give a small wave.

The guys say hello, the girls appraise me. I don't blame them. I'd do the same thing.

Lucas speaks to the group with authority and runs down what's going to happen over the course of the afternoon. When he's done a line forms for the horses. Since I'm a newbie, I stay back, meaning I'm the last to get a horse assigned.

The person who works here walks over the horse I'm to use today, and I take a step back into a hard body.

"He looks angry," I say as two hands clasp on my upper arms.

The horse in front of me is tall and agitated, fidgeting his head back and forth and stepping in place with his giant hooves.

"Have you ever ridden before?" Lucas asks from behind me.

"Yes," I answer, trying to act unfazed by the horse's snarl. "Just not one this big."

"That's what she said."

I chuckle a bit at his joke, and it helps to ease some of the tension coursing through my body.

Lucas sidesteps me, and I miss his hands on my body in an instant. "I'll take him, and you can take the other horse." He points to a smaller brown horse that appears to be only a slightly better option, though the horse seems like a wanderer based on the fact that the people who work here seem to be having trouble reining him in.

"Um . . ." Do I want to be a wimp? Hell, no. "That's okay, I'll take this one." I move forward, straightening my back, willing myself to believe that I can control this beast.

"I like it. I guess you must be used to handling big things," he says and my eyes instinctively veer down to his package.

He chuckles and my gaze shoots back up to his face, and

I know a blush is now tinting my skin. "It's all right. You're not going to hear me complaining if you look." He steps forward, and my breath halts in my chest. "I think I made it clear the other night that I was hoping you'd do more than just look." He drops the octave of his voice so only I hear him.

My thighs clench and I remain as calm as one can be even though my insides feel like a bull waiting for its eight seconds inside the rodeo ring.

"Oh," I say.

Lame, Tahlia. So fucking lame.

"You can let me know whether you're a looker or more of a hands-on girl." He waggles his brows and then saunters toward his horse now that they finally have him ready for Lucas to mount.

Is he asking me for a quick fuck in the back of my BMW, or a longer, more leisurely bang at one of our places? Both fill me with a thrill I haven't known in years—maybe ever.

Lucas swiftly mounts his horse as though it's as natural as driving for him.

"Ma'am." The guy nods my way, and I watch his flexing forearm holding the reins on the horse. The muscles in his arm are straining as if he let up even a little, the horse would rear back.

"Um." I hesitate, and the guy nods for me to go ahead.

Is he crazy? I'd rather not become paralyzed just to find a date.

Lucas and his brown horse trot over, which fuels my horse's adrenaline further. The handler, having no other choice, grips tighter, but the horse rears his head back with a neigh that sends spit spraying across my face.

Chuckles from the group of participants ring out around me. I close my eyes in disbelief and wipe my face. The man still doing his best to grip the reins of the crazy horse in front of me hands me his bandana. I wipe the rest of the saliva off my face and nod to the man in thanks, returning his bandana.

I second-guess my decision to be here. So far nothing has gone as planned.

"Come on," Lucas says, his hand extended waiting for mine.

"I can just sit out." I glance around, seeing that there are a few benches outside of the pen.

"I hate to break it to you, but if you don't do the activities, you're wasting your friend's money, and I don't think you'll win the bet." He cocks his eyebrow, and we both know he has a point.

I grab Lucas' hand, place my foot in the stirrup and he pulls me up effortlessly until I'm straddling him from behind.

I try my best to ignore the scent of his cologne, or the way he shifts to get himself comfortable. He backs into me and pushes the seam from my jeans in exactly the right way to leave me biting my bottom lip.

The workers open up a gate in the pen, and another one of them leads the group of us out. We all follow behind him and his horse in single file.

"There's an awesome spot on the trail where we'll stop and have lunch. It's this really great pond," Lucas says, tapping our horse with his heels. "Good girl, Violet." He pats the side of her neck, and I swear she sighs. I'd sigh too if he were on top of me whispering sweet nothings into my ear.

Violet trots along and I keep my hands on his hips, but once we start moving up into a hilly area, Lucas puts the reins in one hand and eases my hand to the middle of his stomach. "Hang on tight, it might get bumpy."

The front of my body is flush against his now as my hands entwine across his hard-as-a-rock stomach. The scent of his soap mixed with his cologne fills my nostrils now that my nose is practically shoved into his neck, and a little voice at the back of my head warns me this is a terrible idea. He's trouble, but damn, he's like chocolate. I shouldn't indulge, but my willpower is too weak. Maybe just a nibble.

Yeah, right.

THE WAY LUCAS NAVIGATES the horse through the hillside is flawless. It's obvious this isn't his first time on a horse. The rest of the group are still in front of us, riding along the open trail. We stay back, and I wonder if that's because he's the leader and wants to give people privacy, or if maybe it's because he wants the two of us to have some privacy.

"So, you're a boxer and an adventure dating leader?" I ask, and he laughs.

"I'm a boxer." I can actually hear the smile in his answer. "My buddy had some business to attend to out of the country, and I agreed to take over being the point man on all the group dates until he returns."

"Oh. That's nice of you."

"Yeah, I'm good like that." He chuckles again, a deep and hearty laugh that makes my stomach flip. Well, part of the stomach flip might be because I can also feel his stomach muscles contract underneath my hands while he laughs. "Unfortunately, I've been doing it for two months."

"That's a long time. Is your friend okay?" I ask even though it's none of my business.

"Yeah, it's a family thing. He had to go back to Seoul to settle his family's estate."

"Sounds complicated."

"Is there such a thing as an uncomplicated family?"

Just as we're easing into a conversation, we reach the pond. The same handlers from up on the ranch take each horse and tie it up to a wooden post, while everyone else heads toward some tables set up along the water's edge.

Lucas shakes off the help of the handler, putting Violet alongside the wooden post and securing her. He holds his hand out to help me down, and by some small miracle, I don't make a fool of myself while climbing off. I send a mental thanks off into the universe for the fact that Mom and Dad made me take riding lessons when I was young.

"Go enjoy yourself. I have some things to discuss with the workers." He nods his head toward the lunch spread and disappointment turns my stomach because he's not joining me.

"Okay," I say, turning my attention to the people I should be mingling with.

I'm halfway to the picnic area when Aaron approaches me.

"Where were you?" he snips.

I'm put off by his aggressive tone, so I don't bother to fake pleasantries. "How about you lose the attitude." I glance at him from the corner of my eye, but men like Aaron don't understand that you don't bug a woman until she agrees to go out with you.

Aaron walks in line with me to the picnic area. The set-up is cute with red plaid tablecloths and large picnic baskets filled with an array of sandwiches and salads to choose from.

"Sorry, I was just happy to see Lucas didn't keep you for himself. He has a reputation around here."

"Reputation?" I ask.

"Yeah, he likes to pick one girl out of the herd, and he

ends up taking her home after." Aaron hands me a paper plate.

"Is he allowed to do that?" I ask, because I would think that being the leader would come with standards. I push the fact that Lucas propositioned me a half hour ago to the back of my mind.

"He's not a teacher or our boss. He can do whatever he wants." Aaron's tone is filled with ire. It seems someone is not Lucas' biggest fan. "All the women like him because he shows up with bruises and cuts on his face to every event we have on Sundays. You know women and bad boys." He rolls his eyes as he reaches for a sandwich out of the basket.

Actually, I don't know about bad boys. Chase and the few before him were always well groomed and treated me like a porcelain vase in bed. Which seems to have been part of the problem considering Chase probably went to his whores for the rough and kinky.

My eyes waver toward Lucas, laughing it up with the handlers. As if they can sense my gaze, all their eyes veer my way, and I snap my head back to Aaron.

An odd thought occurs to me as I place the last of my food on my plate and begin walking toward an empty picnic table. Are the handlers in on his scheme and I'm the girl he wants this time around? Is that why I got the bad horse, and he took Violet? I had no choice but to ride with him unless I wanted Whit or Lennon to pick me up from Memorial Hospital.

What a little jackass. Well, not little, but he's a jackass all the same.

"You don't seem like the type who goes for that kind of man." Aaron takes the seat next to mine at the picnic table, and a woman who's been wandering from table to table places lemonades in front of us. Another couple sits down across from us. I smile, taking a bite of my pickle.

"I like guys who treat me nice," I say. The woman across from us smiles at my comment.

"Well, as luck would have it I'm nice," Aaron says.

I smile at him, not responding because my mom taught me to keep my mouth shut unless I had something nice to say.

We eat our lunch, and the other couple talks mostly amongst themselves, which is unfortunate as I'm left listening to Aaron run off his resume to me. I hear about his college days on the dean's list and how he's the youngest blah, blah, blah. Before he can backtrack to high school, the staff announces we have ten minutes before we'll have to get back on our horses.

I wipe my mouth, placing my napkin on my empty plate.

"Excuse me, Aaron." I stand. "I wanted to take a walk around the pond."

He stands, and I release a frustrated breath.

"By yourself?" he asks.

I nod.

"Okay. Here, let me." He takes my plate from my hands.

"Thank you." *For the plate and the break from your incessant talking,* I don't say.

"There's a beautiful field of wildflowers on the other side."

He turns and sits back down at the table while I venture off in search of some peace and quiet. The dirt path is worn out of the grass, presumably by numerous people before me.

The quiet allows my mind to wander to the state of my life. What am I truly looking for? Another meaningful relationship like Chase, or a fling with a guy like Lucas? I've never been one to be by myself, but that idea sounds nice right now—to avoid the drama of dating for awhile. But then Whit and Cole flick to mind. How happy they are. Damn, if I don't envy their relationship because Chase might not have been the one for me, but we had our moments. Being part of a couple felt nice.

I round the corner, and the field of wildflowers comes into view, the colors shining and highlighted from the sunshine above. It's beautiful just like Aaron said. I pull out my phone to take a picture when I hear giggling coming from the tree line not far from where I stand.

Someone must be getting it on back here. I tiptoe back and snap a quick picture before I interrupt someone's fun. Following the path back, I spot everyone climbing onto their horses. Violet is still secured along with one other horse. The handlers look at me, and I guess they don't remember who I am because they signal to the other open horse.

Aaron catches my eye and glances over my shoulder before he rolls his eyes almost to the back of his head. I glance over my shoulder to see Lucas walking back on the same path I just left, a pretty girl in front of him. The top two buttons of her shirt are unbuttoned, her lipstick is smeared, and pieces of her hair hang loosely out of her ponytail.

My stomach lurches even though it shouldn't. I have absolutely no claim over Lucas. In fact, there's nothing between us. Even so, the mental images running through my mind of him and that girl still hurt.

He looks over at me with that damn flirtatious smirk.

Without returning it, I climb onto the horse that's not mine and fall in line with the rest of the group.

I don't have the heart to turn around and see his reaction because it'll mean witnessing the other girl behind him on his horse, her hands wrapped around his waist.

I should be glad this happened. It proves exactly why a bad boy isn't a good idea at all. If it hurts this much when I have no investment, what will happen when my heart joins the mix?

EIGHT

TWO NIGHTS LATER I'M seated at my parents' dining room table with my younger sister, Caterina, across from me. She's looking more hippyish than usual today, pushing her bohemian style to the ultimate low.

"Thrift store have another sale, Cat?" I bring my glass of red wine to my lips while she scowls at me.

"I'd rather wear vintage than Louis Vuitton." She forks her tofu and places it delicately in her mouth like we were trained at the Junior Manners Academy from two to fifteen.

"You're the only person I know who buys a bag of clothes for twenty dollars and hangs them in a closet the size of most people's apartments. Way to stick it to the man, Cat." I place my piece of beef wellington in my mouth, smirking the entire time.

Caterina's face reddens, but she's trained better than to raise her voice or throw any sort of a tantrum at the table. The Santora girls are upstanding, well-mannered women who never cause a scene.

"I heard Chase is dating again," Cat sneers, her eyes narrowing across the table.

The Santora girls are not above pushing one another to the brink, though.

"Really?" I concentrate on my knife slicing the meat, imagining it's Chase's heart. Or his dick.

"Yeah. Mallory said she saw him with Quinn."

My knife slips and screeches along the plate.

"Quinn?" my mom asks, and I focus on my plate, unable to show Cat how much her news is affecting me.

Quinn and I have been in competition our entire lives. We were the typical friends-to-enemies story once we hit high school. The end of our friendship was a pivotal moment in my life. Our sophomore year she went to boarding school after her parents divorced, but every holiday when she returned the comparisons between us would be brought up at the country club.

My mom would boost me up and her mom her, which only made us hate each other more. If she wants my sloppy seconds, she can have the asshole.

"Well, I'm sure Linda loves that Quinn is with a Webber." I sneak a glance at her. She serenely places her fork and knife on her plate then reaches for her wine glass and downs a sizable gulp.

There have been times I wondered if my mom wanted me to turn a blind eye to Chase's wandering dick so that she could be related to the Webber family. I'm still not sure.

"I'm done with the Webber name in this household. Find something else to discuss." My dad's authoritative tone straightens all our backs. "We're having a guest for drinks and dessert."

"Oh, yes," my mom says and raises her hand to get our butler Eldon's attention. He comes over, bending over so my mom can whisper in his ear. He nods and then moves back into place.

"Who?" I ask, glancing across to my sister, but she's busy moving her vegetarian meal around her plate.

"Michael Plotter." My dad says the name and then concentrates on his food.

"Who is Michael Plotter?" I ask, because the only people who come to our house for coffee and dessert are businesspeople or close members of our family, and since I've never heard of this Michael, it must be the former.

"A fix-up for Tahlia?" Caterina's eyes light up with amusement.

My dad glances at her and then to me. "He's a friend's son. Graduated from Yale a couple of years ago. The company that was employing him can't afford him anymore."

"And we can?" I ask.

My dad shoots me a warning glare.

Right before I found out what Chase was up to my dad told me business was declining. That like Caterina, a lot of people felt that sausage was too high in fat and too unhealthy now. The public wants turkey, tofu, or any vegan-style dish rather than our quality product. I guess I haven't done my job and sought out answers to combat the problem since I've been too caught up in my own drama.

"Hmm . . . fresh meat." Caterina voices her unwanted commentary on the topic. "Maybe he can put Tahlia in her place." Her lips slide the tofu off her fork before a condescending smile forms on her mouth.

"It's not like that." My dad's forehead creases as he cuts through the meat on his plate. "He's going to go through our day-to-day financials and see where improvements can be made."

"Dad?" I wait to continue until he turns his head to look at me. "I think we could do this ourselves."

"No, Tahlia, we can't. He's highly recommended so give him a shot, okay?" He winks, and I lean back in my seat, my stomach knotting. A new guy, huh? Maybe the problems at work are bigger than my father has let on.

I slide my plate away and cross my legs, contemplating how tonight will go. Do I love working for Santora Sausage?

No. But it's the family business my grandfather started, and I won't abandon my dad. It's not his fault he didn't have boys. God knows Cat isn't likely to follow in his footsteps. I'm all he's got.

Elton walks in, and our housekeeper Marge hurries over, clearing our dishes.

"Mr. Santora, Michael Plotter is here." He bows and my dad waves him in. I lift my glass and begin to drain my wine, knowing I'll need it.

"Wino," Caterina says.

"Tahlia, must you?" my mom chimes in. Chugging alcohol wasn't part of etiquette class.

Eldon sidesteps from the doorway, and when Michael Plotter walks into our dining room, I almost choke on my wine, a small squirt leaking from my mouth, drizzling down my black silk top. Taking my napkin, I discreetly try to blot the stain, but I catch his eyes on me.

Caterina looks at him and then back to me and her eyes widen. "Yummy," she mumbles.

"Caterina, shh," my mom whispers.

Cat is right, though. Michael might as well have stepped out of *GQ* magazine. Hell, he might as well be one of those strippers from Down Under in Vegas that Lennon dragged me to last year. His chiseled jaw leads up to electrifying blue eyes, and his suit sits perfectly across his broad shoulders and trim waist. His entire aura is impeccable from his gelled hair down to his wingtip loafers, and I should be drooling.

I suppose I technically did given the stain on my blouse, but it was because I was expecting some geeky kid my dad is throwing a bone to, but this man needs no bone. Still, the buzz that should feel like the fourth of July in my pants isn't there, my cheeks don't flush, my mouth doesn't salivate. Nothing, nada, zilch.

Nothing like every time I've seen Lucas.

The minute that thought comes into my head I push it away.

Oh, my God, maybe my lady parts are broken from one disappointment after another.

"Mike," my dad says, rising from his chair to offer his hand.

Caterina's eyes are pinging between me and the man candy, like maybe a fix-up would be a good idea after all.

"Good evening, Mr. Santora." Mike shakes my father's hand, and the shiny metal object on his wrist moves up and down. He's the real deal. A Breitling watch probably worth the price of a new car fits snug on his wrist. I glance down at my disappointment of a vagina and still nothing.

"Call me Bill." My dad faces the table, and my mom straightens her back, holding out her hand. "This is my wife, Bree."

Mike slides swiftly to my mother's side, taking her hand between both of his, staring her directly in the eye. "Pleased to meet you, Mrs. Santora." He glimpses me from the corner of his eye, but his facial expression doesn't change.

My mom waves him off with her free hand and releases a small giggle. "Call me, Bree." I swear she sounds like she just finished a spin class.

"My older daughter, Tahlia," my dad says and gestures to me, "and my younger, Caterina."

Mike eagerly turns and holds his hand out to Cat. She glances down and slides her thin hand into his palm. He concentrates on only her for the two seconds they're greeting one another. Once their hands part, Cat practically faints back into her chair, and her eyes zero in on his ass while he rounds the table toward me and I have to work to suppress a giggle.

This man sure knows how to give someone his sole attention and somehow, it's not creepy. He holds his hand out to me, half bowing at the waist like I'm a princess or something. Yeah, right.

"Pleasure," he says, and his tongue snakes out to lick his lips.

His hand covers mine, and I wait for it. The zing, the electricity, the butterflies . . . anything.

My shoulders fall. Nothing.

"Nice to meet you," I say as though it's any other business meeting. No stuttering, sputtering or word vomit. My heart rate is as steady as a lifelong marathon runner's.

His eyes zoom down to my chest and then back to my eyes before anyone else notices.

"I'm hoping we get to work together." He releases my hand, and I bring it to my lap.

"Tahlia is much too busy. You'll be working solely with me, Michael." My dad speaks before I have a chance and that perma-smile Michael's had on his mouth falters for a second before he lifts those corners back up.

"Too bad." He winks and sits next to me.

He unhooks the button of his jacket, sliding into the chair with the confidence of a man who's pulled that maneuver a million times before. It's a practiced move I usually love in a man.

Cat is practically drooling like a Saint Bernard over her alfalfa sprouts, but I'm cool as a cucumber in the refrigerator.

I might as well adopt a cat because I'm ruined.

chapter

NINE

I WALK UP THE pier, my eyes pinned on the yacht Single in SF has booked for the night. A tour of San Francisco Bay and a candlelight dinner are on tonight's itinerary. My heels click on the concrete and my stomach rumbles with nausea because I would like nothing better than my couch, a romantic comedy on Netflix and a pint of Ben and Jerry's.

When my phone dings in my purse, I stop by a lamp and pull it out of my clutch. I slide my thumb across the screen and immediately I know I have no choice but to persevere.

> *Whit: If you need us, call.*
>
> *Me: You going to rent a row boat and save me?*
>
> *Lennon: You could be like Overboard and swim to the shore.*
>
> *Me: She was swimming toward Kurt Russell.*
>
> *Lennon: Fool. Did Kurt really think she'd give up all that money?*
>
> *Whit: It was romantic.*

Me: Money isn't the be-all and end-all, Len.

Lennon: Well, you'd know. I wouldn't :P

Whit: Good luck, Tahl. You got this, girl.

Me: TTYT

I put my phone back in my clutch and glance behind me to the line of taxis, knowing Whit and Lennon would have no idea if I bailed on the cruise. I could easily lie and tell them I went. But I've never lied to my friends, and I don't plan on starting now. The devil on my shoulder says I'm an adult and what do I care what they think? If I don't want to do it, I don't do it. It's simple.

My gaze veers back to the large white boat as people start to line the front of the bow. A few guys stand behind their dates, wrapping their arms around their waist as their cheeks touch. The girls smile out at nothing, and their expressions say they're in heaven.

The knot in my stomach tightens like the rope attaching the yacht to the harbor.

"Are you not coming?" A deep, familiar voice pulls me from the debate going on in my head.

Lucas is standing there in black slacks and a black button-down shirt, the top two buttons undone. Do men realize how sexy that is? He's slicked back his hair and rolled his sleeves up to his forearms. And as always, he's delectable.

I guess my lady parts are in good working order because it feels like someone just filled me with high-octane gasoline and I have to squeeze my thighs tightly together. The knot in my stomach loosens with a flutter.

"Um."

"You were going to ditch, weren't you?" His lips curl up at the corners, and he holds his arm out for me to take.

"Your friend isn't back yet?" I ask, sliding my arm through his.

"Nope." We stroll toward the ramp to the boat.

"I'm sure you're counting the days," I say, but he's quiet for a second.

"I was," he says softly.

I sneak a look over at him, and he's doing the same from the corner of his eye.

"I signed an agreement." He stops us outside the boat and detours us to the railing running alongside the water. His usual lighthearted demeanor is oddly serious and quiet. "I think you probably know I find you extremely attractive . . ." He reaches out and runs his thumb over my cheek. My skin heats under his thumb, and I divert my gaze to the row of boats swaying in the bay. He continues, "But I signed an agreement when I took over for my friend. I'm not allowed to fraternize with the clients. My friend could lose his job, and he's going through so much, I can't be the dick who does that to him." His hand covers mine on the railing of the pier. "I'm sorry."

"You can't fraternize?" I ask, confused. I don't know why because I don't know if I'd even want to date this guy, much less sleep with him. Okay, that's a lie. A part of me—a large part—wouldn't mind seeing how mind-blowing he is in bed, but date? I'm not looking for a replacement for Chase.

"No. But as soon as my buddy returns, I'd love to take you out."

I stare at him long and hard, remembering the girl coming out of the field with bird's nest hair and smeared make-up. "You didn't seem to mind fraternizing on the horseback riding event." I slide my hand from under his and cross my arms over my chest.

Confusion mars his beautiful features before he says, "Liz?" He refers to her by name, and I swear bile rises in my throat.

"I don't know her name."

His head rears back and a boisterous laugh similar to the night at the boxing tournament roars from his throat. "That's why you ran out of there before I could catch you?"

Okay, my heart warms a little with the thought of him wanting to talk to me. Not that I'll tell him that.

"No." I shake my head, unbelievably adamant. "I had an appointment."

He purses his lips and nods slowly. "That shatters my ego a bit, but I'll believe you."

He's so willing to trust me, I almost want to admit how I broke down in my car on the ride home. How I've lost the self-confidence that used to burn inside of me.

"Just to clarify, I caught Liz with one of the ranchers and broke it up. I actually followed you down the path, hoping to spend some time with you when I heard them."

He's so honest it's terrifying to me. Which is ludicrous, because after all I've been through, isn't that what I should want?

"I guess I had the wrong idea."

"I'm serious about wanting to take you out, Tahlia. You intrigue me." He looks me up and down, a Cheshire smile on his lips by the time his green eyes meet mine. "I still don't understand why you're here. You don't need to find a date in an Adventure Dating group."

I shrug, not willing to embarrass myself more by reminding him of what Lennon and Whit already announced at the boxing match—my fiancé cheated on me and the royalty of San Francisco wedding was canceled.

"It's complicated," I answer, and he steps to my side, offering me his arm once more.

"Hopefully my friend returns soon so I can uncomplicate you." He smiles and my insides explode like sparklers just lit.

I don't say anything because what am I going to say? I'm

not about to admit to him that he's the only guy who's excited me since my wedding was called off. That a mouth-watering specimen of a man stood before me a few nights ago, and did absolutely nothing for me. Lucas is the exact opposite of anyone I've ever wanted, but damn if I wouldn't mind him showing me exactly how a woman should feel.

We board the boat, and he walks us into the bar area. I recognize a lot of the people from the horseback riding outing. They're all dressed to the nines—diamonds are glittering, watches are sparkling, and the mixture of perfume and cologne almost nauseates me.

Aaron is standing next to the bar with one of the girls from last weekend and his eyes zoom in on Lucas' and my entwined arms. He rolls his eyes and then focuses his attention on the girl again.

"Sorry," Lucas says and slides his arm out from mine, taking out his phone. "Have a great time, Tahlia. Just not too much." He chuckles and those green eyes of his sparkle with amusement.

I miss him the minute he's gone. I watch his back as he moves between the people checking them in on his phone. The girls seem to make conversation with him longer than the guys and the point Aaron made to me about him picking a girl at every event surfaces again. Lucas could be lying to me about catching Liz and the rancher. It could have been him sleeping with her in the field of wildflowers, but my gut tells me he's honest.

As usual, my subconscious sneers at me because my gut's compass clearly let me down where Chase was concerned.

I make my way to the end of the bar opposite Aaron and order a glass of wine. Needing some air, I take my glass of white and step out onto the front of the boat. Couples still line the edge, and I find a secret spot on the side, away from them.

I sneak a few peeks at the loving couples, a pang of melancholy settling in. I miss having someone in my life. Miss the comfortableness of a long-term relationship like I had with Chase. The way his hand would easily wrap around my back and mold to my side. The easy conversation between us, which now that I think about it mostly revolved around business. The way we knew when the other wanted a kiss.

I would have liked more excitement, sure. Chase never romanced me in any way, but I always chalked it up to the fact that we met right when I was starting college and then we became busy with our careers. I figured one day we'd find the time for candlelight dinners and yacht cruises along the bay.

I'm busy reminiscing about a man I shouldn't waste any more headspace on when I spot someone who looks just like Chase.

I blink. My mind must be playing tricks on me.

Then the guy's head turns to look in the opposite direction, and I'm reassured I'm not a Brittany Spears head-shaving away from the loony bin. Chase is here with his arm around the waist of a brunette who's curled into his chest.

My throat constricts and my mouth goes dry as I watch her rise on her tiptoes and kiss his stubbled jaw. My hand drops to my side, and the glass of white wine hangs from my fingertips while I fixate on the girl who's where I used to be.

"Hey, Tahlia." Aaron comes out of the bar area, blocking my view of the loving couple. It's the only good thing he's done for me since he began hovering the day we met.

"Hey, Aaron." I swallow down my emotions, plastering the smile on my face like my mother taught me. Her words about 'never showing weakness' ring in my head.

"You'll never believe the client I landed this week . . ."

Aaron's voice fades as Chase's hand slides down the woman's arm until her petite hand takes his. I'm not sure how long I'm able to keep up the facade of listening to Aaron, but when I snap my attention back to him, he's no longer bragging about his business accomplishments . . . he's holding my wine glass. I glance down to my shaking hands and clench them into fists.

My eyes reach his, and there's concern there.

"Excuse me," I whisper, turning on my heel to escape this place.

"Tahlia!" he screams out, and I shake my head and wave him off. Hopefully, he gets the hint that I need privacy.

No bet is worth this, so I tuck my clutch under my arm and weave through the throngs of happy couples with the grace of Miss Débutante. I'm five steps from the ramp when a group sandwich me in their greeting. I duck and dodge, but by the time I escape that hell, the boat moves away from land.

No, I scream internally.

More and more space separates me from escape. I look at the edge of the boat and then back to the dock. Maybe I can just jump it? Or fall into the water and swim to safety? I was on the swim team at thirteen.

There's no way I'll survive three hours of watching Chase and his new whatever-she-is. I wonder what happened to Quinn? Or maybe the girl with him tonight is his side piece, not unlike what he had going when we were together. Maybe this woman was with him the entire time I was.

Nausea in my stomach demands my attention as my thoughts run away from me. I clutch my stomach, cover my mouth and run inside the bar area for the restroom.

Sweat beads at my forehead as I turn and lock the door to the small space. It only makes me claustrophobic. I pull my hair into my fist as I lose the contents of my stomach.

I'll stay in here for the whole trip, I think as I flush the toilet and move in front of the mirror to freshen up. *No one will miss me.*

A loud knock sounds on the door.

I pat my face with a towel, staring at myself in the mirror.

"Tahlia," Lucas calls and my heart rate picks up. Am I really going to let this man see me in a state of distress again?

"Hold on," I say, straightening out my shoulders and inhaling a deep breath.

I rinse my mouth with mouthwash and thank God that I thought to put the one-shot travel use in my purse. It pays sometimes to be as prepared as I am. I stick a mint in my mouth and smack on my everything-is-dandy smile and open the door.

If Aaron's eyes were concerned, Lucas's are fierce and protective. He looks me up and down, and this time my body doesn't heat up because he's double-checking to make sure I'm not bleeding or hurt. There's no predatory or lust-filled eyes as he takes in the state of my body. Nope, he's in protector mode.

"Are you okay?" he asks, touching my forearm. "You're clammy." He rubs his hand up and down my arm. And then he raises his hand and places it on my forehead. "Are you seasick?"

I stand in front of him, not answering one question because I'm not about to embarrass myself by telling him why I've now thrown up in his presence twice.

"No. I'm fine." I wave off his concern and push past him to make a beeline toward the bar. I barely sipped that white wine, and I now need it more than ever.

The line is ten deep, and though I know there's probably another bar on the upper level, I glance around. Since I don't spot Chase, I decide to sit tight where it's safe.

Lucas meets me in line. "Are you sure?"

"Yeah, I'm good." I hold my clutch in both hands in front of me as I look everywhere but at him.

"All right. Well, if you don't mind, I'll just keep you company." He stuffs his hands in his pockets and rocks back on his heels.

"Suit yourself," I answer and shrug.

A few of the other adventure daters walk by, nodding their heads or saying hello as they mingle with one another. Lucas is polite, he greets everyone by their first name and shakes every guy's hand.

By the time I'm three people away from the bar, the girl with Chase walks in the sliding doors to my right and I get an up-close look at her.

I shake my head because I should have known. Quinn.

I'm surprised I didn't recognize her before, but I only saw the back of her head, and she's changed her hair since the last time I saw her.

"I take it there's more than just people from Single in SF here tonight?" I ask as my gaze follows Quinn.

She walks through the crowd with poise and confidence. Her dress is conservative but sexy all in one. She's been a thorn in my side and my biggest competitor for a decade, and here she is with the guy I was supposed to marry.

"The company can't fill the boat on their own, so the rest of the tickets sell to the public." He watches me watch her for a moment then asks, "Do you know her?"

I nod.

"Enemy, I suppose?" He chuckles, but he has no idea.

"Why do you say that?" I turn to him, and his nearness makes my heart skip a beat.

"You look like a cougar stalking the prey that's been taunting her cubs." If only he knew.

"No, just a girl I had the displeasure of attending school with. Our moms have a friendly rivalry over which one of us is smarter, prettier, and just better."

My eyes fixate on her as she slides between bodies on her way to the bathroom. The eyes of the men she passes automatically shift her way and my self-confidence wanes.

"Cat fights?" Lucas jokes.

I look over at his easy smile, and for a moment I want him to kiss me. Push Chase out of my head. My eyes dip to his lips and an invisible bubble wraps around us as we each stare at one another.

"Q." Chase's voice pops my bubble and my body shivers.

"I'm sorry," I whisper, stepping out of line. I have to get out of here before Chase sees me. I back up to go try to find some nook and cranny to hide in on this godforsaken boat, but I run into someone. The person spins me around, so I'm facing them. Somehow I must have misjudged where Chase's voice came from because here he is. Smack dab in front of me. I stiffen, and I'm pretty sure all color drains from my face.

"Tahl?" he questions, as though it's inconceivable that I could be out having fun and not still holed up in my condo watching reruns of *Gilmore Girls*.

"Chase," I say, trying to scratch the itch on my neck. My entire body feels like it just erupted into hives.

"What are you doing here?" he asks, glancing over my shoulder. To Quinn, I presume.

"Um." I've never been good at lying, but I better figure out something to say. I refuse to let Chase know that I'm here to try to find a date. I could grab Aaron and beg him to be my co-worker. The whole group of them could be my co-workers, but why would a company take their employees on some romantic dinner and dancing cruise?

"There you are." Lucas' hand molds to my hip as he hands me a glass of white wine.

I look over at him, and his smile doesn't falter. He shifts his eyes to Chase and holds out his hand.

"I'm Lucas. Tahlia's boyfriend."

C HASE STUDIES ME, AND since he knows every telltale sign I have that shows when I'm uncomfortable, I snuggle into Lucas's hard chest and try to imagine how happy I would be if what we're pretending was real. The corners of my lips can't deny how blissful that would feel.

Lucas's hand never wavers, holding steady out between the two. Chase eventually accepts the handshake, eyes narrowed on Lucas, judging and appraising.

"Nice to meet you. I guess word that Tahlia's dating hasn't reached me yet." Chase tugs at the collar of his shirt, and I know he's flustered. Satisfaction has me smiling even more.

"I'm surprised Cole never said anything," Lucas says. "He's the one who introduced us." He withdraws his hand and brings his drink to his lips.

Chase glances at me and then back to Lucas then raises a brow. "Yeah? How do you know my brother?"

I look over my shoulder, wondering when Quinn will appear so that we can get off the topic. She always did reapply her make-up hourly.

"Through his whiskey company." Lucas' lie flies out of his mouth as easy as vomit does for me.

Chase nods and rolls his eyes. Brotherly competition at its best. "Oh, yes, my brother and his hobby."

I want to interject about how Cole is a better man than he is. About how Chase is riding his dad's coattails, he's his lackey, but Cole stood up and did what he wanted to do with his life.

"From what I hear, it's far from a hobby," Lucas comments, his fingers drumming along my hip. Again, Lucas takes a sip of his drink and raises it in the air. "It's good stuff. You should try it." He nods toward the bar, signaling that they serve it here.

I glance behind Chase and see that Aaron spots us. He's standing at the front of the yacht and his eyes zero in on Lucas's hand. His simmering eyes drill into mine, and I'm mentally begging him not to come over here. His eyes shift to Lucas again, and his feet start moving.

I feel my smile falter a little with each step Aaron takes.

"We've all been going on a lot of double dates." Lucas continues the charade, unknowing of the annoying pest who's about to blow everything.

"Lucas." Aaron stops, his hands on his hips, waiting for Lucas to give him his attention.

Chase's eyebrows scrunch as he looks at Aaron, probably wondering who he is.

"Aaron, can you give us a second?" Lucas's tone dictates no sign of distress while I continue to scratch my neck from the itch of hives descending on me.

"No," Aaron says. "I've stood around long enough. Get your hand off of her," Aaron demands and Lucas does remove his hand.

Where's a damn fly swatter when you need one?

"Excuse us," Lucas says, not waiting for Chase and me to answer.

Lucas bypasses Aaron and walks over to the edge of the boat. I can tell whatever Lucas is saying, he isn't that happy. Aaron pokes his finger into Lucas's chest, and Lucas grabs his finger, pushing his arm back.

"Your new boyfriend seems to have a temper." Chase's pompous voice reminds me I'm in his presence.

"A temper is better than an amateur gigolo." I square my eyes at him, but he huffs. As though he wasn't serving himself up like a soup kitchen.

"How have you been?" he asks with what sounds like genuine concern.

Like I'm going to tell him that I watched every one of my favorite movies at least ten times over the past six months and refused to socialize unless Lennon and Whit kidnapped me.

"Good." I glare at him, changing my stance.

"I'm glad. Tahl, I am sorry."

I could do two things here. Rail at him for dating Quinn or show indifference.

"Don't worry, Chase. Our breakup was for the best." I purposely let my eyes drift toward Lucas, who is now poking Aaron in the chest.

"I miss you," Chase whispers and my head whips around to find him a step closer to me.

"No, you don't." I tuck my clutch under my arm, ready to flee away from his area. That swim in the bay doesn't sound so bad right now.

"I do." He reaches out, and I turn my body, shrugging off his affection.

He huffs again, shoving his hand into the pockets of his slacks. "I was so stupid, Tahl. I should never have done the things I did. We were so young when we met, and I got cold feet."

I can stand here and be the polite and well-mannered Tahlia I've been trained to be, or I can finally stand up to Chase.

My heels click forward, just as someone from the crew announces dinner. Good. Over the noise of everyone rustling to make it to their seats, no one will overhear me.

"Still a liar, I see. You're forgetting something . . . when people get caught cheating, once everything is out in the open, people start talking. I had friends call me up to say how you hit on them. Other acquaintances told me how you slept with them and they wish they stepped up and said something. So you can take your sorry excuse for a dick and go fool someone else, because I'm done."

Chase's Adam's apple bobs up and down.

"Tahlia Santora?" Quinn's sickly sweet voice breaks the silence.

I step back, and she winds her arm through Chase's. "Quinn. How nice to see you. And with Chase. Wish I could say I'm surprised."

Quinn purses her lips. She can't deny that she's sloppy seconds to me. Especially after Chase's revelation to me a second ago.

"Who are you here with?" she asks.

Chase points to Lucas, and I glance over, crossing my fingers he's not in an altercation with Aaron again. To my surprise, Lucas is sauntering back over to us, his eyes brimming with excitement. He is one fine specimen, and even Quinn can't argue that.

"Him?" Quinn says, and for a moment I fear they know each other, but I quickly remember Lucas saw her already and didn't recognize her. "Where's his jacket?" she asks, grasping for any minor infraction she can pounce on.

Before I can answer, Lucas's arm slides around my back as though it's the most regular occurrence for us.

"Sorry about that, baby," he says, his lips meeting my temple. My entire body flames with heat.

"I hope everything's all right?" Somehow, I keep my voice steady.

"Everything's great." He directs his attention to Chase. "We're here with an adventure dating group."

Did he really just divulge that? I'm seconds away from hopping overboard, I swear.

"Tahlia, you're resorting to dating sites to find a man now?" Quinn laughs, covering her mouth as though she's trying to hide her amusement, but her smug grin is front and center.

Chase joins in her laughter.

"Not us. I'm helping a friend out tonight and I asked my number one to join me." He pulls me closer to his hard body, and again his lips kiss my temple. "Besides, why would Tahlia ever need a club to find a date?" Lucas leans in closer to the center of our tiny group as if he's about to share a secret. "It's a full-time gig chasing guys away from her when we're out. I'm half-tempted to chain her to my bed. I'm sure Chase can relate." He winks and that flame from earlier just ignited into an inferno with the image of me chained to his bed.

Quinn makes some squeaky noise as though she's offended and Chase's eyes zero in on me.

"I did always find her chatting with some guy when we'd meet for drinks or dinner." A small crease forms on his forehead.

"Well," Quinn interrupts and straightens her back. "We should go to dinner." She nudges Chase forward.

"Pleasure as always," I say, waving goodbye.

"I'm sure we'll catch you after the meal," Chase says.

"We'll probably bolt as soon as the boat docks. You know Tahl, she can't ever get her fill, but I'm up for the challenge." Lucas' fingertips dig into my hip, and though my first instinct is to protest I manage to keep my mouth shut. It wouldn't be the worst thing in the world for my ex-fiancé to think I'm having earth-shattering sex on the regular.

Chase looks at me, no expression on his face because he's probably thinking to himself how I was more likely to be changing into my pajamas and tucking myself into bed after a night out while we were engaged.

"Nice to see you, Tahl," Chase says, as Quinn pulls him along.

Eventually, they both disappear inside, and I let out a relieved breath. Lucas swings in front of me, his hands still on my hips as he backs me to the edge of the boat.

"What are you doing?" I ask. His eyes burn with so much fire and desire that my nipples peak under the fabric of my dress.

"I'm going to kiss you," he says.

"I thought it was against protoco—" I never finish because he slams his mouth down on mine. His tongue doesn't wait for permission, but slides through my parted lips, mingling with mine.

Oh, my. His mouth tastes of the whiskey he was drinking. I grab hold of his shirt, pulling him closer. His right hand skims up my side, goosebumps following in his fingertips' wake, and then his fingers entwine in my hair and he holds my lips to his. As if I'm going anywhere. I moan.

His hand loosens on the back of my neck, and he begins to pull away, but I'm not ready for us to come back to our senses, so I lock my leg around his. A groan rumbles up his throat, and he deepens the kiss, pressing the large bulge in his slacks into my stomach. My leg tightens to stop my knees from shaking because his lips are like nothing I've ever felt before.

A chiming song rings out over the boat's speakers, and we're tossed back into the cold water of reality. My leg loosens, he lets the strands of my hair go and no longer do I feel his arousal pushing at my bellybutton. My lips are swollen and bruised by the time his hand snakes forward, his thumb massaging my cheek.

"Better than I imagined." He stares down at me with lust-filled eyes.

"It was all right." My lips betray me and turn up.

"Bullshit." He grips my neck again, and I wait for another breathless kiss, but someone calls out his name.

"It's time for dinner," one of the waiters says.

"Thank you," Lucas answers and turns his attention back to me. "I should probably get you fed before I expend every ounce of energy out of you."

"Oh, I have plenty in reserve."

He chuckles, linking his hand with mine. "After meeting your ex, I'm pretty sure you don't know the real meaning of being taken to bed. We might have to work up to it."

"Are you making a promise, Lucas Cummings?"

He stops us right before the sliding doors into the dining room. With his hand locked with mine, he stares at me for a second. "I think I put up a good fight. It's been harder than spending twelve rounds in the boxing ring." His lips lift and excitement bubbles inside of me like a poured champagne glass. We enter the dining area and step across the deck toward the only table left.

"Yeah, that hour must have been super hard for you," I joke, but again he stops, and when his eyes meet mine, they've grown serious.

"I've wanted my hands on you since you picked me as the underdog to win that fight. Believe me, my hand and imagination aren't doing it for me anymore."

I don't remark, mostly because I'm about to jump into his arms and beg him to drag me off to the bathroom to get rid of this incessant ache between my thighs. So not Miss Débutante.

"Okay," I muster, and he chuckles, releasing his hand to place it on the small of my back.

He leans close to my ear, and shivers run up my neck. "It

turns me on when I fluster you."

I glance down, and sure enough, he's shifting to disguise his hard-on.

"It's all you, Tahlia. Look out to the sea of women here."

My eyes veer around the dining area—everyone is in conversation, sipping their drinks and starting their meals. There are lots of gorgeous women here, though none of the men are as mouth-watering as Lucas.

"None of them do it for me," he says. "Only you."

Then his hand slides down and lightly pats my ass.

"Let's get this dinner over with, so I can really smack your ass."

I swallow deeply and take a seat on my chair—all while my panties soak through.

WE'RE SEATED AT TABLES of four for dinner, and it's uneventful and feels like it lasts entirely too long. Would it make me pathetic if I pretended that Lucas was choking and gave him mouth-to-mouth? Probably, so I sit there quietly, listening to the men talk about sports while the girl across from me chimes in with facts and statistics. I bow down to her if she learned all that useless information just to impress guys. *Well done, sister.*

Lucas' hand roams under the table to my thigh a few times, but he never takes it far, even though my skin burns to feel those callused palms slide under the hem of my dress. Once we sat down, the man who wanted to spread-eagle me on the table so he could eat me for dinner turned into Mr. Stiff.

Thankfully, the other couple seems to be hitting it off. At least, they're doing that whole flirting about fighting over opposing teams. I've never been into sports. My dad would sit in his study on Sundays and watch the games and Chase would host Super Bowl parties every year, but I think the betting thrilled him more than the actual game.

I glance over at Lucas, and there's a burning desire in his eyes as he discusses whether the Forty-Niners or Raiders are the superior team. I'm at least attuned enough to know they're both California teams. Well, at least Sarah, the other girl at the table, mentioned it about a half hour ago.

As the three of them go back and forth, my eyes veer to the other diners. My mind wanders to Chase and Quinn. How long have they been dating? The only thing that upsets me about them together is that she thinks she's one up on me. Our competitiveness has transferred from our mothers to us in the years since junior high, unfortunately. I should be the bigger person and not care what she's doing with her life, but it's hard not to want to put a girl like her in her place.

Lucas's hand lands on my thigh, and he squeezes it gently, dragging me back to the present. I glance over, and he raises his eyebrow in question.

I smile. Can he be as sweet as he seems?

He stands from the table, pushing in his chair, and I watch him, wondering what he's doing.

"I forgot, there's some paperwork for you to fill out." He motions with his head toward the patio. "I better have you complete it before I forget." Then he looks over to the other couple, who aren't paying either of us any attention. "We'll be back."

I place my napkin on the table, stand up and slide my chair back into the table. I can feel Aaron's eyes on me the entire time I follow Lucas out of the eating area.

The sun has descended, leaving us under a dark sky with a million twinkling stars scattered above us. Lucas leads me to the front of the yacht, then motions for me to take a seat on the bench. I sit down and cross my legs, staring out at the skyline of San Francisco.

He sits next to me, and his arm rests along the back of the seat, his fingertips teasingly close to my skin. Skin that still simmers from the earlier kiss we shared.

"It's a beautiful city," he remarks, and I nod to confirm my agreement. "How long have you lived here?"

It dawns on me that I know nothing about him, and beyond what he overheard the night of the boxing match, and then what he witnessed tonight, he knows next to nothing about me.

"My entire life. You?"

"Me too. Well, I moved out of state for high school and college, but returned shortly after."

I nod. "Where did you go to college?"

His back stiffens, and he stares ahead instead of zeroing in on me like they have been. "Boston. You?"

"Stanford. Family pedigree."

His eyes shoot to mine, and he stares at me for an uncomfortable beat. It's not the usual heated stare, it's filled with curiosity.

"You come from a long line of Stanford alumni?" he clarifies the question I just answered.

"Yeah. All the way back to my great-grandfather. So, of course, I followed in their footsteps. Chase went there, too, so the decision was easy."

I remember how excited I was when Chase asked me on our first date. What a fool I was.

"What's his last name? He looked familiar to me somehow," he says.

I'm caught off guard by this, but it's not uncommon for Chase's face to be in the press from time to time. "Webber. You might have heard of his family."

"I think everyone in San Francisco knows the Webbers." His long fingers tap on his pants and his comment further piques my curiosity because yes, the Webber name is known, but I'm pretty sure Lucas and Chase aren't running in the same social circles.

"He's actually Cole's brother. You know the Webbers?" I

ask, shifting my body to face him better.

"Nah. My dad worked at one of their restaurants and I chatted with Cole once at one of the fights, but I didn't realize he was a Webber. I only know *of* them."

I release a breath because if this boxer is some rich frat boy, then I might as well move out of state to get away from all the Chase clones because nothing about this man says spoiled, entitled egomaniac.

"Does that relieve you?" he asks, his face bent down, so he's right in front of me.

I bite the side of my lip, contemplating his question. Does it? I'm sure there are high-society guys who aren't cheating bastards like Chase. There's Whitney's boyfriend, Cole. And a girl I went to college with, her husband actually changes their kid's diapers, so I'm sure there's is an exception to every rule.

"It does. There's something about a guy who doesn't expect the world to fall at his feet."

My answer earns a smile that reaches right up into his green eyes. His arm drops and his fingers lazily roll up and down my shoulder. "You're shivering," he mumbles, and his muscular body slides closer.

"Aren't you worried someone will see us?" I ask, glancing around, trying not to concentrate on the warmth seeping into my body from his thigh touching mine.

"Nah. The only problem is Aaron, but he won't say anything after our conversation." Now his whole palm is rubbing along my bare upper arm, and he has to know those aren't shivers, they're goosebumps.

"What was that conversation all about?"

He releases a breath and looks over to me. "I probably shouldn't tell you this, but a few weeks ago, a girl got spooked about Aaron. He's sort of on probation, but it'll be up to my buddy when he returns on how he wants to handle the situation."

"Spooked?" Aaron's an annoying gnat, there's no question, but he doesn't seem harmful.

"There was a member who I think liked him until he kept showing up at her doorstep after she allowed him to walk her home one night. I'm not even sure he meant to scare her, I think he's just one of those guys that get attached really fast."

"You mean you won't be showing up at my doorstep tomorrow morning?" I joke, and Lucas glances over at me from the corner of his eye.

"Like I said, Aaron didn't mean any harm, but she reported the incidents, so I ended up having to take her home after one of the dates and then tell Aaron he was never to show up there again. It made her uncomfortable, and I didn't much like the whole scenario."

"Oh."

"So Aaron was trying to tell me to stay away from you and rambling on about the rules. I think he thought I slept with that woman. We cleared the air tonight, so it should all be good."

"Thanks. You didn't have to tell me all of that. I appreciate your honesty." I clamp my legs tighter together, hating the stall of our conversation.

"I didn't answer your question about showing up at your doorstep." Lucas' tone drops a few octaves, and he leans in.

"I was joking."

A smile tilts the corner of his mouth. I try not to return it, but he makes it hard.

"So you don't want to know if I'd show up on your doorstep tomorrow morning if you allowed me to take you home tonight?" he asks, and I don't know how to answer. Am I capable of just having fun without overthinking things?

"Only if you want to tell me," I say in a soft voice.

His hand covers my interlaced fingers on my lap.

"If you let me see you home tonight, I think I can pretty

much guarantee that I'd still be buried deep inside of you in the morning. So no, I wouldn't show back up, because I'd still be there."

That flare of heat in my neck rushes like a raging wildfire straight to the center of my thighs. I swallow the saliva pooling in my mouth, unable to answer, but then again, he didn't ask me a question. Did he? Maybe he did. Is he asking me to have sex tonight? Do I want to have sex tonight? I glance over at him. Yeah, I wouldn't mind it. Wouldn't mind it? I'd love it, and I'm positive he could make me come more times than a football team at a Vegas brothel. He could be my unicorn cock.

Oh. My. God. I can't believe I just referenced Whitney's stupid analogy. That stupid thought that there's one unicorn cock out there for every girl.

"Tahlia." His voice pulls me from my frenetic thoughts.

"Yeah," I say, warily meeting his gaze.

"I wasn't looking for an invitation."

Of course, he wasn't. I mean, he's probably like a Tim Tebow. Lucas is probably just a hotter-than-hell boxer who is saving himself until he gets married. Then again, a devoted Mormon doesn't kiss a woman like he kissed me. And I don't even follow sports so why do I even know that little fact about Tebow anyway? *Shut up, Tahlia. Relax.*

I release a laugh that does nothing to match my words. "I know that." I wave him off, hoping it comes off as casual and not full of all the nerves threatening to take over my rational thinking.

"Would you like to take me home?" he asks and waggles his eyebrows.

My eyes widen. "What? No! I mean. Yes. I mean—"

He places his finger over my lips. "Sorry." He chuckles. "When I see you flustered, it turns me on. I'm being selfish by prolonging your torture." He smiles and I stare into his amused eyes. I say nothing more and he leans in even closer. "You can use me to forget him," he whispers, and the cool breeze isn't affecting my hot body now imagining everything he'd do to me.

"He's forgotten," I answer, my classic answer, and he cocks that damn perfectly arched eyebrow again. What kind of guy has perfect eyebrows?

He shakes his head. "No, he's not, but I'm willing to sacrifice myself for the cause."

"Oh." All the thoughts from earlier run through my head with new fears entering the mix. Did I shave? Yes. Thank goodness Whitney dragged me to the spa the other day and we each got the works. Otherwise, Lucas would have to ask for a map of Yellowstone to find my damn clit.

"Tahlia." His voice again pulls me back to this conversation. "Do you want me as much as I want you?"

All my insecurities and fears race through my mind again and to stop the runaway train from gaining any more steam I blurt out, "Yes!"

Lucas seems momentarily stunned, probably because of my eagerness so I try to save what little face I can.

"I mean, I'm down . . . with everything you said. But I'd prefer if we went to your place."

Lennon's teachings on one-night stands rings through my head. She says when possible always go back to their house. That way if they're a shitty lay they have no way to track you down after, and you can see if the guy is a complete freak based on his place right from the get-go. Besides, Chase was the only man who I've ever had over at my place, and I'm not sure I'm ready for another man to share the same bed Chase and I did.

"So it's settled then. Don't worry." Lucas squeezes me into his side. "I'm more than up to the task." He arches a brow and the live band begins playing a slow melody from the upper deck as I send a small prayer up begging God to make Lucas a man of his word.

TWELVE

THE YACHT DOCKS AT the pier and Lucas purposely has us hang back, so we're one of the last couples off. I appreciate his effort in trying not to advertise the fact that we're leaving together, but it's given Chase the opportunity to wait around until we step off the yacht's exit ramp.

Lucas' hand clenches mine harder as he approaches.

"Can I talk to you?" Chase asks.

I glance over at Lucas, whose expression hasn't changed, and then back to Chase.

"Where's Quinn?" I ask.

"She's in a cab on her way home." He stuffs his hands into his pockets and rocks back on his expensive loafers.

"I'm sorry, Chase, but we're leaving." I squeeze Lucas' hand and step forward.

Chase reaches out and grabs my elbow. "Tahl," he pleads.

Lucas' hand twitches in mine and when I glance over at him there's a storm brewing in his eyes. He looks like he's about one second away from losing his cool.

I slide out from his grasp. "No, Chase. I'm here with Lucas.

If you'd like to talk, call my office."

I face forward, ready to leave him behind me once again, but he grips my arm a little firmer this time.

"Tahlia?" His tone is questioning as though he's confused as to how I'm not caving and giving him what he wants right now.

I swivel around, but Lucas' hand leaves mine, and I know before I turn to see them chest to chest that this situation is volatile.

"She said no." Lucas puffs his chest out a little and watching the two of them so close, their differences couldn't be more noticeable. Chase's build is slimmer, and everything about him screams money and white collar, whereas Lucas' broad shoulders and superior height shadow Chase, along with his more rough-and-tumble vibe.

"Back off, Johnny-come-lately," Chase baits. I'm sure if he knew Lucas was a boxer with the name Raging Bull, he might have thought twice about his remark.

"When a lady tells you to leave her alone, you do," Lucas says, and Chase narrows his eyes.

"She wants to hear what I have to say." Chase's eyes linger my way with a softness I recognize from days long past, and for a moment, I'm about to intervene and allow him five minutes of my time.

"Let me guess," Lucas bites out. "You want her back because you saw she moved on? Maybe you'll convince her, and you'll head over to your current girl's apartment for a quick fuck before the two of you actually get back together."

Man, it's scary how much Lucas knows Chase without knowing him.

Chase places both of his hands on Lucas' chest and pushes him. "Mind your own damn business. She's my fiancée," Chase says, and all the air in my lungs swooshes out.

Chase's words have my feet cemented to the ground. How

much I loved those words. Loved being someone's fiancée. Loved being committed to someone else with the promise of a future.

Lucas steps forward with his fist cocked back, but I push myself between them, one hand on Lucas' muscular chest.

I shake my head at Lucas and he lowers his arm. I turn and face Chase, but Lucas remains right behind me as though he's my bodyguard and paid to protect me.

"Chase." I take a moment to consider my words and compose myself, so he won't know how affected I was by his last remark.

He smiles that cocky, arrogant you-know-you-want-me smile, which only helps me come back to reality. The one where he moved from bed to bed to bed.

"Tahlia," he soothes, and Lucas groans behind me.

I cut him off before he can continue. "It's ex. I'm your *ex*-fiancée," I declare. "And Lucas isn't my boyfriend."

Chase's eyes sparkle with a satisfied arrogance and he glances behind me to Lucas.

"I am a member of the adventure dating group. Whitney and Lennon bought me a month pass because they're sick of seeing me on the couch. Sick of me wasting time pining over our relationship. You know what? The more I think about our relationship, it wasn't so great. You came and went as you wanted. I lied to myself, telling myself that you were busy making a name for yourself at your dad's company. When I look back and dissect each moment of our long relationship, I think on some level I knew. I think I just chose to ignore it. You may have ruined my trust in men, and when I do date another guy again, he'll probably pay a little for the damage you've done, but I can tell you one thing for certain. You will never be that guy."

I step back, and Lucas grips my upper arms to keep me afloat like a life vest in the middle of the ocean. My shoulders deflate and he accepts my weight until I'm able to gear up for another lashing from Chase. Because he won't accept failure easily.

"You're ruining your future. At least find yourself someone who will be able to support you," Chase sneers, his eyes moving up and down Lucas. "I could've given you everything. All the money, all the clout, the lifestyle you're used to. You think you're going to leave your dad's company now? Forget it, sausage queen. You'll be supporting guys like him for the rest of your life." His face is beet red when he motions to Lucas.

The pressure of Lucas' hands wanes and another groan leaves his lips. If I thought the episode at the boxing ring was embarrassing, this is downright period-stain-on-white-pants-in-high-school horrific.

Lucas slides by me and separates Chase and I. "I think it's time for you to go." Lucas' cool amazes me. You'd think he had a temper, being a boxer and all, but his heartbeat is probably steadier than mine at the moment.

"Whatever. Happy living in your shack, Tahl. I'm sure your parents must be thrilled with the recent changes in your life." He turns and walks away.

Bringing my parents into it was a low blow, even for Chase. I step forward, to do what exactly I'm not sure, but Lucas pulls me back into him and his arm swings around, his hand molding to my hip.

"Let him go," he says softly.

We both watch as Chase walks down the pier to a waiting taxi. He opens the door, and there sits Quinn staring back at me. Once he slides in and the car pulls away from the curb, my body relaxes, but I don't have much of a chance to think because Lucas' lips crash to mine and again, he's walking me backward until he locks me against the railing.

I've never felt so much intensity from one kiss. My knees are weak, and my body feels like a firecracker whose fuse was just lit. By the time he ends the kiss, and we regain a somewhat normal breathing pattern, I barely recollect what just happened.

"My place, right?" he asks, and there's no sweetness left in his voice. His domineering caveman tone implies that he's ready to drag me down the pier at top speed and chain me to his bed.

"Yes." I nod, and he nods and then we're walking. Fast. His hand is raised in the air to hail a taxi ten steps before we reach the curb. He opens the door, I slide in, him beside me and when we're both secure he rambles his address to the taxi driver.

It's all moving so fast, and I barely have time to think before the cab pulls off the curb and his hand slides up the hem of my dress. His touch quiets my jumbling mind.

I waited all night to feel those rough fingertips graze my upper thigh and a jolt of anticipation runs from my toes to the top of my head. I squirm but then his voice is in my ear. "Relax." The sweetness in his voice is back. He nudges my legs to uncross and then nudges some more until they part. "A little more," his soft voice instructs.

I open, and his fingers run down my damp panties at a slow, measured pace. My head falls back onto the vinyl of the seat. The fabric chills my neckline as the cool spring air rushes past my face from the open window.

I'm thankful for one thing—this cab driver listens to loud talk radio. I lift my head an inch and pry one eye open, finding the driver peering up and down from the rearview mirror. I close my legs, but Lucas slides closer, his hand deeper between my legs, pushing them apart more and more and again my head falls back.

"Did I make you this wet?" he asks in my ear as he nips at my earlobe.

I nod. He slides my panties over, and I bite my lip to stop the long moan that wants to escape. His finger moves down my center, coating my wetness up and down until he concentrates on my clit. His thumb circles it, he sucks my earlobe between his lips and my senses speed into overdrive. He's going to make me come in the back of a cab.

"Relax. Let it come," he whispers. His hot, warm breath tickles my ear lobe.

I squirm and push my chest out, needing him to touch my heavy, aching breasts.

"Later. I promise you, your tits will get plenty of attention tonight."

His words, his fingers, only bring my orgasm closer. His thumb concentrates on my clit with the perfect amount of pressure and he pushes one finger inside me. My legs move to close, but he shakes his head in the crook of my neck.

"No," his gruff voice says, and I relent, opening to him again.

He pushes another finger in, arching it until it hits my G-spot, and holy shit. I'm not sure anyone has ever hit my G-spot before because I know I'd remember this.

I buck into his hand, his pace quickens and he casts kisses along my neck as he whispers over and over again to relax, enjoy, and he promises what he'll do to me back at his apartment. Promises of many, many orgasms in many, many different ways.

The wind rushes into the car faster as we're speeding down the freeway and his fingers feel like they're keeping pace because I explode onto his hand at the same time his mouth covers mine and he swallows my moan. I ride out my orgasm on his hand, my breathing shallow, my heartbeat hard.

I'll remember this for the rest of my life. I just got fingered in the back of a cab, and I know for Lennon that's probably like getting coffee in the morning, but to me, it's something huge. Something I never thought I'd be able to relax enough to do. Something tells me that Lucas could get me to agree to just about anything.

"Jesus, you're hot," Lucas whispers, bringing me back to the here and now, placing a chaste kiss on my temple. "I can't wait to feel you tighten around my cock."

His fingers slowly leave me and then he positions my panties back in place, pulls down the hem of my dress and he puts one of the fingers in his mouth and sucks.

Just like that I'm ready for round two.

THE CAB PULLS UP to a white building on the outskirts of town and at first, panic sets in. I've accompanied a virtual stranger to an undisclosed location where I agreed to get naked with him so he can do whatever he pleases with me. Maybe I should have booked us a room at the Ritz. At least there would be people around to hear my screams for help.

Lucas pays the cab fare, opens the door and waits for me with an outstretched hand. I don't move, wary of what this place is. The street is vacant with no signs of life and the way the moonlight hits the white concrete building makes it look a little creepy in contrast to the dark sky.

"Um," I mumble and the driver's gaze darts to mine in the rearview mirror. He's probably wondering what my problem is since we were obviously into each other on the ride over.

Lucas bends down and the trustworthiness in his green eyes dispels my worries for a second—until my eyes flick to the building again. This time I notice a sign that says BOXING. That's it. No business name, no neon light, just the word boxing painted on a piece of wood. Maybe boxers don't do neon lights?

"Tahlia." Lucas' soft and gentle voice pulls me back from my racing mind. His gaze moves to his hand and then to me again. I need to relax. It will be fine. I'll be fine. Lucas has done nothing but treat me with respect up to this point.

"Can I have your phone for a second?" he asks and I hear an exasperated moan from the front seat.

"Why?"

Lucas slides back in and the cab driver downright groans this time, not trying to hide his displeasure. "I'm trying to make a living here, you two. Every Uber driver in the city is busy stealing my business," the driver says.

Lucas reaches into his pocket and hands him another twenty, then turns to me and holds his hand out once again.

"I won't leave the car with it." His finger crosses over his heart in a grade-school promise.

I dig it out of my purse and hand it over to him. His thumb slides and I admire his fingers fiddling around. Then he holds the phone up to his ear.

"Hey, is this Tahlia's friend?" I lean forward to listen to the sound of the voice, but he holds me back by placing his hand on my shoulder and leaning toward the window more. "No, she's fine." I hear yelling and I'm guessing he called Lennon. "I promise, she's safe. I just wanted to let you know she'll be spending the night at my place. I live at 3 Cobble Drive. My name is Lucas Cummings and my phone number is . . ." He continues to ramble on facts about himself while the voice on the other end remains quiet. "I had a three point three GPA in high school. Damn Physics." Now laughter is pouring out of the phone. He's charmed her. "Nice talking to you, I'd like to take a ride in your unicorn van sometime . . . yes, of course, with Tahlia." He looks over at me, his gaze roaming over my body. "Oh, I intend to . . . she's not just beautiful, she's scorching hot, stunning." His tongue slips out of his mouth and he licks his lips. "No worries there, she'll definitely understand what multiple orgasms mean when we're done." He chuckles and my face heats.

Without a doubt it has to be Lennon.

He ends the call and hands me the phone.

"Lennon?" I ask.

"Yeah. Now your best friend knows where you're at for the night." He steps out of the cab and holds his hand out. "Join me?" he asks.

"Please join him," the exasperated cab driver says and I roll my eyes before accepting Lucas' hand.

The cab driver speeds off the moment my foot hits the curb and the door is closed.

"Why not Whit?"

Lucas looks down at me, wrapping his arms around my waist, about to kiss me.

"What?"

"How come you didn't call Whitney?" I ask again because she was the last person I called on my phone.

"I thought she might cockblock me. She didn't seem like my biggest fan when we met." He smirks. "Lennon seems like the type who is protective of you, but willing to let a bad guy like me do very naughty things to you."

I step into his embrace a little more, my breasts pushing against his hard chest.

"I'm not sure you're such a bad guy," I whisper as though there are more than sewer rats near us.

His hand splays across my back and he pulls me flush against his body, leaving not even a centimeter of space between us. "You might want to revisit that thought in the morning." He sucks his bottom lip into his mouth for a second and my body rushes into overdrive. I'm ready to find out exactly what I signed myself up for.

He grips my ass and lifts me up until my legs are wrapped around his waist. "Now, tell me . . . have you ever been spread open on ropes?"

I act as though I'm unaffected by his question and I catch his lips forming a teasing smirk. "Not that I can recall."

"Well then, let's see what you think." He walks us to the white building, fishes around in his pocket, inserts his key into the lock and opens the door. Not an easy feat with a full-grown woman wrapped around you, but his strong body moves around as if I'm barely weighing him down.

Once we're inside Lucas lets me drop to my feet and I glance around. It's pitch black but the smell of sweat permeates my nostrils. It's not gross body odor or a foul smell, it's manly. A smell where you feel safe, like if a pack of wolves were circling around us, he'd fight each one off before the vicious animals got one sniff of me. Maybe that's a little extreme, but you get where I'm coming from.

I step forward and Lucas flicks the lights on. My heels click on the concrete floor as I saunter around, examining the studio. There are two rings and a ton of equipment that resemble pieces in my own gym, a gym much cleaner than this one.

"This is where you work?" I ask, my hand brushing along one of the ropes in the ring on my right.

"I own it," he answers.

I spin around on my heel, surprised he hadn't mentioned it before, and I find him sitting on the edge of the other ring. "You do?"

He cocks an eyebrow. "Surprised?"

I shake my head. "No. I just . . . I didn't know." I walk toward him, thinking that if he sees my eyes, he'll know that I'm telling the truth and not being a snotty little rich girl.

"It's fine. I get that we're in two different worlds." His knuckles whiten as he grips the edge of the ring.

I step into his open legs, but he doesn't move.

"That's not what I meant. I thought that you made most of your money fighting." I place my hand on his cheek, the stubble of his scruff rough against my palm.

"I'm getting older. I won't be able to fight forever." There's a note of melancholy in his voice.

His hands remain planted on the ring, so I let my hand drop from his cheek. I step back, but he swings his legs out, urging me back toward him. I almost fall into him, but he catches me. Then before I know it he's lifted the rope and I'm lying on my back in the ring with him half on top of me. He plants his hand on my cheek and turns my head at exactly the right angle so he can kiss me exactly how he wants.

His lips are demanding and urgent on mine as his tongue slides into my mouth. My hand weaves through his long strands while he twists his body, urging me to scoot forward into the middle of the ring as he crawls on his hands and knees, his mouth glued to mine the entire time. Without warning he lies on top of me, the press of his erection firmly between my legs, and I moan as his lips close the kiss and his tongue paves its way along my jaw and neck.

"Hands up," he mumbles, locking them above my head. "Just like that."

He releases the hold on my hands, trusting I won't betray him, which is becoming more and more difficult the further his lips venture down my body. Right now, his mouth is right above my breast line. His fingers maneuver to the right side of my body and he slides the zipper of my dress down. An electric tingle races across my skin. One by one he takes my hands from above my head and slides the straps of my dress down before returning my hands to their previous position. I raise my back to allow him to pool the fabric around my waist. His feasting eyes zoom in on my breasts covered in a black, lace strapless bra.

The color of his eyes deepens to evergreen. He slowly licks his lips. My entire body is humming for him, and I squirm underneath his appraisal, needing to feel his hands on my aching body.

His fingers graze down my chest and he pulls the lace down until my breast pops free. One minute he's examining my body as he reveals it and the next his teeth are playing with my nipple and his tongue is swirling it around in his hot, wet mouth. My legs widen further, and he presses his rock-hard length into me. If I thought my panties were soaked before, they're drenched now and my need for him to be inside of me is more potent than ever.

"Sit up," he demands and his smoldering gaze on mine might just make me crumble into a wanton mess right here.

I sit up a bit and he unhooks my bra, letting it fall between us. He picks it up and tosses it aside. Then he rocks back on his heels to stand and holds his hand out to help me up.

Once I'm standing, he pushes down the fabric of my dress and it ends up in a pile of silk at my feet. I step out, slipping my heels off in the process. His hand winds around my neck and he smashes his lips to mine as his other hand pushes down under my panties and he grabs a handful of my ass. He urges me up until my legs are wrapped round his waist and the hard ridge of his cock pushes against my swollen clit.

Our kiss quickly becomes frantic, our teeth knocking, our tongues sloppy, unable to get enough of one another. My back hits the padded center of the corner and Lucas ends our kiss. He draws back, eyes raking over my body.

"Put your arms here." He lays them on the top rope and then takes the middle rope and winds it over the top of my wrists in a way that effectively binds me there. "Now the legs." I raise my legs up to the bottom set of ropes and my toes clench around them. Thank goodness I work out six days a week.

He steps a good distance away from me and his fingers move to his belt. He slips out of his loafers, taking his socks off, too.

His fingers easily unbutton and unzip his pants and they thump to the ground, his eyes on me the entire time. His hardness tents his white boxer briefs, but my mouth waters waiting for him to finish unbuttoning his dress shirt. That too falls to the mat, leaving him in only his boxers.

His chest heaves and I swear his erection swells twice its size as he stares at me. Normally, I'd feel uncomfortable, but my body heats for him and I want nothing more than to have his hands on me, his mouth sucking on me and his hard length inside of me.

He takes a step forward.

"You're perfect." He slides one side of his boxers down.

Another step.

"Perfect tits." He slides the other side of his boxers down.

One more step.

"Now, I need to see your perfect pussy."

He slides his boxers down his legs and steps out of them.

I suck in a breath as I take my first glance at his fully naked body. His cock is bigger than any other I've seen before. When I say other, I mean Chase *and* the vibrators Lennon's brought over. I lick my lips and realize that for the first time in my life I really *want* to fall to my knees and take a man into my mouth. I *want* to taste him, to feel him at the back of my throat and to feel him wind my hair through his fingers as he explodes inside my mouth.

His hands skim up my legs and grab both sides of my panties, ripping them along the seams.

"Lucas," I sigh. My breasts are heavy with need and my nipples tighten so much it's almost painful.

"Just as I thought, perfect pussy." He falls to his knees, his hands gripping my inner thighs to keep me in place.

Then his mouth is on me, his tongue is sliding along my center and I'm bucking against his mouth. He releases a deep growl from the depth of his throat and I clench to keep my orgasm at bay, not wanting him to stop.

He sucks my clit into his mouth and the scratchy ropes mark my palms from my tightening grip.

Just as I'm about to let it go, assured he'll get me here a second time, he stops. His tongue licks up my stomach, through the crevice of my breasts, up my neck, over my chin to my lips.

"I need to be inside of you," he whispers and before I have a chance to kiss him again, his lips leave and move to my ear. "Be right back," he says.

He jumps out of the ring and the light overhead is too bright to see what he's doing away, but he returns seconds later, with a condom.

"Miss me?" he asks.

My eyes fixate on his hands as he opens the condom, takes it out and places it on the tip of his dick. My mouth doesn't just water, it practically salivates like a cartoon character's.

I want to scream at him to hurry, I want to grab him and bring him to me, I want to guide his cock into my pussy so he can fuck me so hard our eager bodies are slapping against each other slick with sweat and I'm no longer Tahlia, the obsessive-compulsive prude, but his sex kitten purring for more.

Before I have to beg, his arms move under my thighs and we both watch as his massive length slides into me. To my surprise we're a perfect fit. The stretching sensation around his cock amplifies as he drags himself out of me and I clench around him.

There's nothing sweet or gentle about our sex. It's raw, it's intense, and it's electrifying. He controls my hips as he thrusts again and again. Since my arms are secured to the ropes he takes a step back and pulls my body out from the corner of the ring. His large hands clasp my hips while he drives his cock in and out of me. He's in complete control and there's nothing I can do except take it, enjoy it, bask in the pleasure he's bestowing upon me.

My breath is shallow and my heart beats wildly in my chest. My clit is engorged and the tingling sensation begins in my core and I know I'm close.

"Fuck," he murmurs, his eyes closing as I begin clenching around his cock.

"I can't hold it," I manage to say.

"Don't. Come all over me, baby."

Once 'baby' flows out of his mouth, I'm done. No one has ever called me a term of endearment like that and I'm not sure why it carries me over the edge, but I freefall over the cliff Lucas brought me to.

He reaches forward and releases my hands from the ropes.

"Lucas," I cry out and he only pumps faster and harder into me. I ride the wave of my orgasm as long as I can, spiraling into bliss and unwilling for it to end.

"Wrap your arms around my shoulders," he says, his voice breathless, and he locks my back against the cushion and continues fucking me like the beast he is. My breasts rub along his bare chest, teasing my nipples while he licks and sucks on my flesh. He jerks into me out of rhythm and then moans out his release.

"Perfect. Fucking perfect," he mumbles until he stills inside of me and his shoulders relax slightly.

I wait for him to release my legs, to back up and dispose of the condom, but he keeps us where we are. His lips move up to my lips until he kisses me slow, gentle and more loving than I would have thought he would. He ends the kiss and then his arms unhook, letting my weak legs fall to the floor.

"Stay the night?" he asks before we're even disconnected from one another.

"Sure," I answer, not sure that I should, but knowing I don't want to leave him right now.

"Let me clean up and then we'll move this upstairs to my

apartment," he says, pulling out of me and grabbing his boxers on the way under the ropes.

I pick up the shreds of my panties and then put my dress on, no bra. Tucking them into my purse, I grab my phone and glance up to double-check that he's not on his way back here. I see a text from Lennon, of the damn graphic she had made up of the unicorn cock for her t-shirt.

Lennon: I have a good feeling about this Lucas guy.

I think he's your 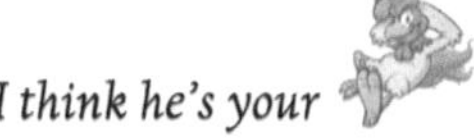

I laugh, but for once I wonder if Lennon might know what she's talking about.

FOURTEEN

I WAKE UP, FEELING the delicious soreness in my body from a night of sex. Not just regular sex, but mind-blowing sex. Don't get me wrong, I've always enjoyed sex, but I now understand why people can be preoccupied and addicted to *that*. I'm not sure I'd ever have enough of Lucas. Last night we did it again in the shower, he bent me over his kitchen table, and lastly at six this morning, he woke me up by sliding his cock inside me. The feeling that he wants me as much as I want him is thrilling. Unbelievably so.

His fingers brush along my side and I'm thankful it's Sunday because if I had to go to work right now, I think I might actually cry and throw myself on the floor in true toddler tantrum fashion.

I moan and his lips follow the path of his fingers as he makes his way down to my pussy. Sooner than I'd prefer, his head emerges from the sheet and I smell myself on his lips. In only one night I realized something about Lucas—he loves for me to kiss him after he goes down on me and to lick his fingers after he's pleasured me with his hand. He loves when I taste myself. It spurs an unquenchable desire in him that I'm more than happy to fulfill.

"I literally have no energy," I say, my arms falling to my sides.

His deep chuckle vibrates off my neck and his green sparkling eyes cast down to me.

"Coffee?"

Although I can't bear the thought of his body lifting off me, I know staying in bed all day is not an option. Plus, I'm not sure I've done that since . . . um . . . never. Never have I spent the entire day in bed. Santora women don't lie around. Too much to be done.

"Sounds amazing," I answer and just as I suspected, I miss the weight of him when he leaves the confines of the bed in order to make our energy-replacing drink.

He swings his legs over the bed, leaving me to admire his perfectly sculpted back while he shimmies his boxers on. Not sure why he wants to wear clothes now—he didn't earlier when we raided the fridge at three am. Then again, I ended up pinned to the counter as he had me close my eyes and fed me a variety of takeout.

His apartment is a small studio, so I admire the way his strong body moves around the space while he makes coffee. Quickly, the smell emanates throughout the room, awakening my tired limbs. I sit up further in the bed, trying to find my dress, but I spot it in a ball by the front door. Nope, not sauntering across this floor for it even if the man knows in full detail what lies under the sheet I'm clutching to my chest. What is it about daylight that brings all your insecurities back to the surface?

One of Lucas' t-shirts is balled up in a chair sitting next to his bed, so I slide out from the covers and throw it over my head.

"Caught you," he says, jumping on the bed. "Why so shy?" he asks, his finger lazily moving up and down my arm.

"I'm not shy." I stand and pull the t-shirt down even though it hits me mid-thigh. It smells like his cologne—a musky scent mixed with what I now know from our shower last night is his soap.

"You're leaving the bed." He scoots up to the headboard, his hands resting in his lap, not an embarrassed bone in his body. I wouldn't be either if I had less than ten percent body fat.

"I need to use the restroom." I glance over my shoulder and rush to sneak away.

While in the bathroom, I hear him moving around the apartment. Hard rock music starts to play soon after and I contemplate my choices. I have lunch plans with the girls, but I could cancel. The only thing I *have* to attend today is my family dinner tonight. Sundays at the Santoras are never to be forgotten. Then I realize I'm assuming he wants me to stay. Maybe coffee was out of pity, or his way of saying, *Here's your coffee, you may go now.* Maybe he's nice like that, so I don't have to stop at Starbucks and be one of many girls doing the walk of shame home.

Knock, knock.

I startle, turning the knobs on the faucet off.

"Coffee is ready," he says and his footsteps pad away down the small hallway.

"Be right there."

My fingers weave through my hair to get the snarls out. Lucky for me, there's no bed head since my head was only on a pillow for maybe an hour total the entire night. I dig through his drawers for toothpaste, coming to a stash of unused toothbrushes. All inscribed with Dr. Audrey Campbell, DMD. Nice, either he's a thief or he's screwing Dr. Audrey Campbell, DMD. I select a pink one and if his hidden toothbrushes are for all the women he brings home, it's a nice touch. Like a parting gift at the end of an evening. I imagine a group of girls talking. "Oh, Lucas Cummings makes sure you never leave his place with plaque on your teeth or bad breath. Every visit comes with a complimentary toothbrush!" What if every guy handed something out after a casual sex night? The possibilities are endless.

Knock. Knock.

"I'm getting lonely," he says.

I brush my teeth as fast as possible and place Dr. Audrey's pink toothbrush on the side of the sink. I open the door to find Lucas leaning against the wall with a cup of coffee in his hand. He hasn't put on any more clothes and there's a small bulge in his boxers now.

I reach for the cup but he raises it above his head.

"I need payment first." His face is stone cold and shows no sign of amusement.

I walk up to him, my t-shirt-covered breasts pushing against his hard chest, rise on my tiptoes and place my hands on either side of his face. My lips plant on his and he sneaks his tongue into my mouth, deepening the kiss. After a few minutes, I drop to my heels and he hands me the coffee.

"I see you found the toothbrushes?" He smirks.

I nod, walking down the hall. "Nice parting gifts," I say. I swivel on my feet to face him and he has a puzzled look on his face.

"Breakfast?" he asks, opening his fridge door. I doubt he can cook for me since last night he fed me his leftover takeout from the week. Cold pizza, lo mein, spaghetti.

"Pizza?" I laugh and he closes the door, grabbing his own coffee and sitting next to me at the table.

"Yeah, sorry, last week was my binge week." His hand pushes through his hair and I miss the feel of his silky strands already.

"Binge week?"

"Yeah, I train hardcore for my matches and then I allow myself to binge for one week."

"Why? You don't seem to have to worry about weight?" I

take a sip of his coffee, realizing it's not my usual.

"I have to stay within my range otherwise I won't be allowed to box." He focuses on me and I have no other choice but to swallow down the black coffee.

"When is your next fight?" I ask, placing the cup of coffee on the table again. Lucas' gaze tracks my movements and he leans back in the chair.

"Three weeks."

"How long have you been boxing?"

"Why aren't you drinking the coffee?" He eyes the full cup again and looks at me.

"Oh, I was just talking." I go to pick up the cup again, but he swipes it out of my hand and places both of the cups into the sink.

"Come on, we're going out." He nods for me to stand and walks over to his dresser and pulls out a pair of black athletic pants and tosses them on the bed before opening another drawer.

He's insane if he thinks I'm going to put on the dress I was wearing last night and go out for breakfast.

He turns around when he senses me still sitting down at the table.

"No one will judge you where we're going. You want to borrow something?"

I stand, moving toward my now wrinkled dress. "If something of yours fits me then it's me who will have to watch my weight." I grab the dress and move toward the bathroom to change, but Lucas stops me.

He plants his hands on my shoulders and peers down at me. He's still in those boxer briefs.

"Let me look at you one more time." He says it like a direct order, not a question, and a small burn ignites between my thighs.

Both his hands grip the hem of his t-shirt and, so slowly it's painful, he raises it up my flesh until he removes it over my head. He doesn't lay a finger on me as his gaze singes my skin, slowly taking in every part of my body. I shift my stance, hoping to quench the desire that's building.

Lucas takes the dress from my hands and holds it out for me to step into. He spins me around, zips me up in the back and then he swipes my hair off my neck and kisses where my neck meets my shoulders. My nipples pucker under the silk of my dress.

I close my eyes, knowing that I want more of him. One night is not enough.

"I'll be right back," he says and I hear him move into the bathroom.

He emerges a few minutes later with Dr. Audrey's toothbrush in his hand.

"You don't want your toothbrush?" He chuckles and I can't read him well enough to know if he's serious or not, but I take it from his hand, shove it in my purse and wait by the front door until he's ready to leave.

FIFTEEN

W E WALK DOWN A flight of stairs that I don't fully remember walking up last night. When we step out onto the road the California sunshine lights the street and it looks completely different than last night. Cars line the curb, businesses have OPEN signs on the doors and people are walking the sidewalk with coffee and newspapers in hand.

"What a difference from last night," I say.

"Yeah, it truly is night and day around here."

His hand rests on the small of my back as we venture down the street. When we cross, I spot a diner with a line outside and I assume this must be where we're headed.

"This place has killer cinnamon rolls," he says close to my ear as we take a spot behind a family of four. The wife eyes my crinkled dress and Lucas' sweats and t-shirt. I try to ignore her when she rolls her eyes and elbows her husband.

"How many have you eaten in one sitting?" I ask, leaning my back on the brick building.

He laughs. "Six."

"Six? That doesn't seem so bad."

"Wait until you see how big they are."

With that our conversation stalls slightly as we continue to step forward in line. Suddenly, I'm uncomfortable about this whole next morning routine. How does Lennon do this? Maybe we should have stayed at my house. At least I have food in the fridge and clean clothes. I wouldn't have seen the stash of toothbrushes he has for his sleepover guests and feel as though I'm one in a long list of women.

"Hey," he says, discreetly planting a kiss on my shoulder.

I turn my head and he gives me another quick kiss.

"What?" I ask.

"You're thinking way too hard." He winks. "Did you forget him?"

His question brings the reason he asked me to go home with him last night front and center. I did forget—not once did Chase or Quinn cross my mind the entire night.

I smile. "I did."

"Then my mission is a success."

My lips dip for a second before I realize I'm showing my disappointment. "Thank you," I say, plastering a smile on my face.

"You're welcome." His smile reaches his eyes. He's obviously proud of himself.

Thankfully, the hostess grabs two menus and shows us to our seats. I need the moment to remind myself that Lucas isn't the type of guy who does serious. Hell, I'll be lucky to spend another night with him.

We sit in the back at a booth for two and the waitress pours us two cups of coffee. I put my two sugars and dash of milk in the cup, stirring it with a spoon. Lucas's phone rings and he pulls it out of his pants.

"Excuse me," he says, stands up and walks to the restroom area.

The waitress comes over and places a cinnamon roll on

the table.

"Oh, we didn't order that," I say to the waitress who has yet to say two words to me.

"This is Lucas' usual on Sunday morning." With that comment, she walks away, taking the order of the family sitting across from us who just happen to be the family that were in front of us in line. The little girl at the table continues to stare at me and I shift on my vinyl seat, wishing she'd turn her attention elsewhere. She's probably only six, but I swear there's judgment there.

Lucas returns a few minutes later, sits down and smiles.

"Sorry. That was my friend." His smile widens. "The one who leads the adventure dating. He'll be back in two weeks."

I nod. "That's great. Then you'll be done."

He picks up his coffee. "Thank God. I swear one more lame date and I was about to jump off a bridge." He sips his coffee and I unwrap my silverware, placing my napkin in my lap.

"I can imagine," I mumble, cupping my coffee mug.

"Oh, great, the cinnamon roll came." He eyes it and then nods my way for me to have the first bite.

I mentally add 'feed them cinnamon rolls' to Lucas' morning-after repertoire.

"No, thank you," I say, my gaze darting over to find the blonde girl staring at me again. Now her attention is pinging between Lucas and me. Her mother tries to divert her gaze away, but we must appear like a car accident you can't help but look at. I'm starting to feel like we're a car accident because as soon as we left the cocoon of his apartment, things started going south.

Picking up his fork and knife, he cuts a piece off and holds it up to my lips.

I shake my head and he pushes it closer, the icing hitting my lips.

I shake my head again.

He frowns then turns the fork his way and places it in his mouth.

"Is something wrong?" he asks, putting the silverware down.

"No." I sip my coffee again.

The waitress taps our table. "One more second, Lucas."

He nods absently at the waitress, but keeps his gaze on me. "You seem upset."

I glance across and the little girl is still watching me. "Is this your usual Sunday morning routine?" I ask the question before I can stop myself.

I might not understand all the rules of casual dating, but I'm fairly sure one is not to be upset the next morning when a guy wants to buy you breakfast.

"Excuse me?" He leans back, not understanding my question.

"This. The toothbrush, the cinnamon roll the waitress knows to put down before you even ordered it. You know, where all your walk-of-shames are fed before you release them back into the wild."

He sits there, calm and cool, and as edible as the lemon meringue pie in the glass case at the front of the diner.

"What does it matter?" he asks and I uncross and cross my legs again, sliding my ass to the back of the cushion to straighten my back.

"It doesn't." I wipe my mouth with the napkin and place it next to my coffee cup. My hand lands on my purse and I'm about to slide out of the booth when he raises his foot to the edge of the booth to stop me.

"I think it does." He raises those perfect eyebrows.

"Let me out," I whisper-yell, my blood heating in anger. "Why?"

I lean over the table so he can hear me. "I'm sorry, this is my fault. I should have warned you. I don't do casual, and I'm unfamiliar with the parting gifts and the morning-after cinnamon rolls. Sitting here, I realize that I can't do this."

"Do what exactly?"

"This whole 'you screwed me senseless last night and now we're going to have coffee and ignore any possibility of doing it again.' It isn't me." I slide again, knocking into his sneaker, but he doesn't budge.

"So you didn't get enough of me last night?" he asks, a smirk across his lips showing me how amusing he finds this.

His question throws me for a second before I realize his foot has dropped off the booth. The cocky grin on his face does it. My silk dress slides along the booth and I'm standing at the edge of the table with my clutch tucked under my arm, my chin held high as if it's every morning that I'm in a wrinkled dress with sex hair and no make-up on.

The waitress comes over, eyes the confrontation in front of her with her pen and pad of paper poised to take our order and just stands there waiting to see what happens next.

Lucas's eyes don't leave mine, humor filling the green hues and his lips teasing a smirk.

"Thank you for a great night." I nod and swivel on my heel.

"You sure you don't want the cinnamon roll?" he calls out to me and I stop, the waitress' eyes boring into me again.

Turning around, I grab the cinnamon roll and leave the diner and Lucas Cummings behind.

chapter

SIXTEEN

"**H**OLD ON!" I SCREAM as water drips off my body onto the hardwood floors of my apartment as I run to the front door.

I open the door to find Lennon's smiling face.

"I told you I'm done with my experimenting phase," she says, bypassing me in my towel, inviting herself into my apartment.

I follow her into my living room and she plops herself on my couch, putting her feet up on my coffee table.

"Make yourself at home." I walk to my bedroom door. "I'll be right back."

"I'll be waiting for all the juicy details."

"Get your feet off my table," I holler out and shut the door to my room.

After I get dressed and comb out my hair, I walk out to my living room to find that Whitney has now joined the party.

"You girls are early," I say, moving toward my coffee pot.

Whitney and Lennon stand from the couch and come to sit down at my breakfast bar, each holding their own mugs, having already helped themselves.

"Did you really think we'd wait around for you to offer up the deets of your wild night of abandon?" Lennon smacks the counter like a judge's gavel. "So . . ."

"It was nice," I say. "Until this morning."

"Did he ask you to drop off his dry-cleaning when you left? Disappear early and leave you in his apartment like Cole did to Whit? Did you wake up in his childhood room surrounded by trophies and gaming systems?" Lennon rambles on and I don't even want to know if these are things that have happened to her. "Once I knew this girl who was so smashed that she woke up with his mom staring down at her. He still lived with his parents. They fucked on his SpongeBob SquarePants sheets!" She looks over at Whitney, who is struggling to swallow her sip of coffee. "Can you imagine?"

Whitney strangles down her coffee and then bursts into laughter. "Are you sure it wasn't you?"

Lennon huffs as though she's offended but holds up her hand in the air in the Girl Scouts' honor sign. Everyone knows she was never a Girl Scout. "Swear. It was Tina Reynolds."

Whitney and I share a look like, *Whatever, it was so Lennon.* Then they both direct their attention back to me and I feel as though there's a spotlight over my head and I prepare myself for the interrogation to come.

"So . . ." Lennon starts as usual. Whitney props her elbows up on the breakfast bar and rests her chin on her hands.

"I may have had a minor freak-out at the diner this morning." I lean against the counter and cross my ankles, bringing my coffee to my lips to distract myself.

"Diner? As in breakfast? He took you to breakfast?" Whitney asks with a that's-so-sweet tone and a smile teasing her lips.

"Yeah." My voice is so low with embarrassment that it couldn't be heard by a dog, much less a human being.

"That means you were more than a booty call, girl." Lennon raises her hand for me to high-five her, but I shake my head.

"I think I ruined it." I sip my coffee again.

"How so?" Whitney asks.

"Um . . ." Both their eyes are zeroed in on me and my voice catches in my throat. "I didn't know what to do, what was appropriate behavior after a one-night stand."

"Appropriate behavior?" Lennon says with a fake British accent. "Why, Lucas, a lady never kisses and tells." She raises her pinky while she sips her coffee.

Whitney knocks her with her elbow to stop and then focuses in on me.

"I just . . . I was with Chase for so long. He's the only man I've ever slept with. I've never done this whole casual dating thing. Then I found these toothbrushes and the waitress brought us a cinnamon roll." I begin to ramble but they get lost the longer I speak.

"Oh, man, a toothbrush and a cinnamon roll. You're right. There's no coming back from that." Lennon eggs me on and I slam the coffee cup down on the counter, the caramel liquid overflowing.

"I'm going to die with twenty cats around me. They'll probably gnaw at my body once I can't put their food out anymore."

"Don't be so dramatic, Tahlia. One of us would find you first," Lennon jokes, trying as usual to lighten the mood and make me laugh.

"You guys will be off with your grandchildren or something." I wave a hand at them.

"Grandchildren? This body is not meant for procreation." Lennon raises her arms for us to look her over. She's probably right, but not because of her body. I'm not sure the girl could ever settle on one person long enough to make the commitment to have children with them.

"By then Cole and I will be empty-nesters and you can live with us, but no cats, Cole's allergic." Go figure, Whit's the one to actually put it in a realistic scenario.

I stare at the two of them, tearing off a paper towel to wipe up my mess. I throw away the dirty paper towel, refill my cup only to find the two of them looking at me again. This time with pity.

"So, seriously, what happened? It sounds like it was going great." Whitney leans back this time, sipping her coffee. "Let's start with the good stuff."

I blow a long breath out. "The good stuff." My smile emerges full-wattage as I picture all the ways Lucas took control over my body last night. "He's amazing in bed. Nothing like Chase."

"Chase aka selfish lover." Lennon adds in her two cents.

"Oh, I forgot to tell you. We ran into Chase." I place my coffee down, climbing up on my counter because I know they'll want to hear this.

"What?" Whitney screeches.

For the next twenty minutes I tell my two best friends everything that went down last night. How Chase was with Quinn and that he wanted to speak to me and how Lucas pretended to be my boyfriend so I could save face.

"What a douche." Lennon's face contorts like she just drank sour milk.

"What about Lucas though?" Whitney is quick to keep the Chase train from running off course. Thank goodness.

"Lucas is sweet, hot, good with his hands. No complaints in the sex department."

"I could tell by his voice. He has a voice that could make you wet just hearing it," Lennon remarks and I hope that didn't happen last night.

"This morning he made me a horrible cup of coffee that

I tried to swallow down with no complaints. But he could tell, so he took me to a diner."

"So far so good." Whitney waves her hand to keep going.

"We had to wait in line and there was this family in front of us. The daughter kept staring at me and the mom looked disgusted. I started to feel dirty and whorish."

"Whorish?" Lennon clarifies.

"You know what I mean. I had on my dress from the night before and he was in sweats. My hair wasn't a rat's nest, but it still had that just-fucked vibe. Anyone could figure out what had transpired between us."

"That's their problem."

I release a long breath again. "I'm not you, Lennon. I freaked. I found a stash of toothbrushes under his sink."

"His parting gift?" Lennon asks.

"Exactly." I point to her. "Is that a thing? Like do men give the women things before they leave?"

The two of them stare at me again and burst into laughter.

"No." Lennon shakes her head. Her tone suggests that I really am clueless. "No, they don't."

"It's like a courtesy then?" Whitney chimes in, ecstatic she has the answer correct. She's not exactly the girl with a long list of one-night stands.

Lennon shoots her the same bored weirdo look. "No. They're probably for the girls he sleeps with, but it's unusual. My finger and his toothpaste are my usual morning-after routine."

We both nod.

"Continue," Whitney says.

"I took the toothbrush thing to mean he has a steady stream of women in and out of his apartment. Then we're seated and the waitress just lays a cinnamon roll on the table while he was taking a phone call by the cashier."

"How dare she?" Whitney says, giggling.

Ignoring her, I continue. "I told the waitress we hadn't ordered it and she said, 'It's his usual.'"

"Where is the diner?" Lennon asks.

"Across from his apartment."

"Safe to say he goes there a lot?" Lennon asks.

I shrug, embarrassed. "Probably. He mentioned how good the cinnamon rolls were while we waited in line."

"You have to wait in line to get in?" Whitney asks, her eyes lighting up.

"Yeah."

She pulls her phone out. "What's it called? Those are the best places. I'm going to ask Cole to take me there next weekend." Her fingers are poised ready for the four-one-one from me and I glare at her for the fact that the best short-stack pancakes are what's on her mind in this moment. She tucks her phone away. "Sorry, carry on." Her head shrinks down into her shoulders.

"Anyway, I don't know. Everything started adding up in my head and I didn't know what to do. I panicked thinking he was just waiting for me to cut loose. And . . ."

"You did. You left him at that restaurant to eat the cinnamon roll all by himself?" Whitney asks, her lips turning down like he's the kid at lunch with no one to sit with.

"No."

"You didn't?" Lennon asks with a smile.

"I took the cinnamon roll with me." I bury my head in my hands, the heat of my embarrassed flush covering my body.

"He didn't even get the cinnamon roll?" Whitney asks, her lips turning true pouty. "Bad, Tahlia."

"Nope. I ate it on the way home in the cab," I confess with shame like I'm a closet over-eater at a Weight Watchers' meeting.

The two of them burst out laughing, Lennon slapping

the counter, Whitney's gaze moving from me to Lennon and back again.

"Was it as good as he said?" Lennon asks between chuckles.

"I'm glad that my life is so humorous." I hop off the counter, take the final sip of my coffee and place the cup in the sink. "I have to do my hair."

I leave the two of them in my kitchen while I walk into my bedroom. I'm unwinding the blow dryer when Whitney peeks her head in through the door.

"Sorry," she says. "Can we come in?"

I nod and the two enter the small confines of my bathroom. Lennon takes a seat on the toilet lid and Whitney hops on the counter.

"I'm sure it wasn't as bad as you think," Whit tries to assure me.

I cock my eyebrow at them and they snicker a laugh.

"Seriously, Tahl. He sounded nice last night and like he only had the best intentions. Who else would take the time to call the girl's friend to get her out of the taxi?" Lennon remarks and I guess she's kind of right. "I blame myself for this. I should have prepared you more. I failed as a teacher. I've let you down on your journey to singledom."

I plug in my blow dryer. "I'm twenty-six, Lennon. I should be able to handle a casual hook-up."

"Look, we forget that you've been prepared your entire life. You went to etiquette school, débutante school. Your mom has never let you just walk into a situation without you knowing exactly how you're supposed to act and what you're supposed to do. Casual sex is a beast for even the most prepared. It's my fault I didn't tell you that there are no parting gifts handed after and that if the guy attempts to make you coffee, that's a good sign." She smiles and I laugh at myself.

"I bet he calls," Whitney says.

"I never gave him my phone number," I remark with a frown.

"If he wants to see you again, he'll find a way to get your number." Lennon's lips quirk up into a smile and I hope for once she's right.

SEVENTEEN

MY ASSUMPTION IS THAT Lucas didn't want to call. It's been five days and nothing. Isn't the rule three days or something?

"Miss Santora." A deep voice pulls me from my internal debate on where I heard about the three-day rule in the first place.

Michael Plotter leans against the door frame to my office with a smile across his face. He places his computer bag on the floor just inside the door, walks into my office without asking and plops himself down in the chair in front of me.

I sit up straight in my office chair, crossing my legs, and try to appear like the professional I am, not like a girl trying to figure out why a boy didn't call her.

"Lunch plans?" he asks, his eyes dipping to my cleavage and back up to my eyes.

"I don't take lunches." I tap my pen on the desk.

"You don't eat?" he asks. He brings his leg up to rest his ankle on his knee. His movements are suave and effortless.

"I eat. I just don't leave the office."

"Let's order take-in then," he offers. His fingers strum the arm of the leather seat.

"Mr. Plotter, why would I want to have lunch with you?" His gaze never veers away from mine so I hold his stare.

"Why wouldn't you?" His phone vibrates in his pocket, but he never pulls it out.

"Because I have a lot of work to do here." I eye the files that Midge, my secretary, just brought me.

"I bet you work way too hard, Miss Santora." He takes a moment to pull out his phone to see who was calling.

"It's my family's company, of course I do."

He nods. "I think Santora Sausage can spare you for an hour." He stands, tucks his phone back in his jacket pocket. "I hate to eat alone."

"I don't suppose you're alone often." I comment, standing to see him out.

He chuckles. "True." My stomach growls and he eyes it and then raises his eyebrows at me as if to say, *Stop the act.*

"Fine." I relent because I have no argument now. Plus, I was supposed to have lunch with a client who canceled last minute. "You're buying though." I shrug on my raincoat and grab my purse.

"I'd have it no other way," he says behind me before we walk out of my office.

Midge glances at me as we pass her desk and when she spots Mr. Plotter behind me and she does a double-take. There's no doubt he's a male Adonis. He's just not my type—anymore.

"I'll be back in an hour, Midge."

"Yes, Miss Santora." She nods. "Mr. Plotter." She nods again.

He continues behind me to the elevators and I press the down button.

"What exactly are you doing for my father?" I ask him, still annoyed I've been kept in the dark.

The elevator arrives and we file in with a few other

employees, so I stop the business talk.

A familiar scent hits my nostrils and my eyes casually cast over the people in the four-by-four space as though he'd be standing in the corner. It's the same cologne Chase used to wear, I know it, so I scour each person as they come and go on each floor.

"Looking for someone?" Michael asks softly in my ear and I draw back to gain some distance.

"No," I say, my two hands clenching my purse in front of me.

The elevator stops at street level and I file out with everyone else for lunch. The streets are busy with people trying to grab their lunch before having to return to work, so Michael holds his hands up for a cab.

"Corridor, please," Michael instructs the driver and the car pulls away from the curb.

Michael is busy on his phone most of the trip, frantically emailing or texting, I'm not sure what, but his thumbs are sliding along the screen at max speed. I could pull my phone out and stare at the blank screen again, but I'd rather not. I take the opportunity to study him. I wonder what he's like in bed? His well-built body implies that he'd be good, but he could be selfish or inexperienced. What am I saying? A man with ocean-blue eyes and a strong jaw like him is definitely experienced in the bedroom.

While the cab stops and goes in traffic, I find myself comparing Lucas and Michael. They come from different worlds. One's rough, the other smooth. One wears a metal chain around his neck of the St. Christopher medallion and the other one an expensive watch. If I close my eyes, I can still feel the coolness of the metal hit my heated skin as he ground in and out of me. The way it slid up and down between my breasts. How the small piece moved with him and teased me as much as his lips and tongue.

Someone touches my arm, jolting me back from my memory.

"Tahlia," Michael's soft voice says.

I shake my head, plastering a smile on my face.

"Sorry."

He smiles but he's hesitant and I really hope I wasn't moaning out loud while I was daydreaming.

I follow him out of the cab and while he pays, I look up at the restaurant, thankful he didn't inadvertently choose one of the Webber families' holdings. Michael picked the perfect place for a dreary day in San Francisco. After the rainfall this morning, the dark clouds stayed behind, blocking any sun. Corridor is known for their comfort food—pastas, risottos and meatloaf. My mouth is watering just thinking about the food hitting my belly.

Michael's hand lands on the small of my back and I step forward faster to shake it off. That's intimate and I'm not giving the guy who is supposed to be just a co-worker the wrong idea only for him to be upset about it later. He seems to get the hint, opening the door for me to enter first.

The somber male host seats us at a table that's set up along the glass window overlooking the street outside. Michael pulls out my chair and slides it under me as I sit down. I place my purse on the back of the chair and shrug out of my jacket. Michael takes off his coat, hanging both of our coats on the hooks next to the tables. He sits down to join me.

I'm not sure what to call this. It's not a business meeting, nor is it a date. I tell myself to just go with the flow.

"What are you doing for my father?" I ask him the question I attempted to earlier in the elevator.

He places the menu down on the table, leans forward and clasps his hands together.

"I'm helping you guys stay in the black."

There's something sketchy in his expression. Not endearing as I'd hoped. More like, *You guys have screwed the company up and I'm going to fix it.* I don't like it and I'm thinking there's a whole other reason why I'm seated across from him right now.

"Why are you the right person to help us?" I ask, my tone turning bitter.

"You went to Stanford, right?" He leans back now, a cocky grin taking the place of the flirtatious smirk he wore earlier.

"Yes."

He nods his head like it's good but not good enough. "Yale," he says and points at himself.

"Yeah, I heard. How old are you?"

He narrows his eyes, trying to decipher why that matters. "Twenty-five."

"And at twenty-five, you've come across a lot of companies where you have the knowledge and experience to help them increase profitability?" I lean my elbows on either side of my chair rests to show how relaxed I am and that he's not going to get a reaction out of me.

"The last company I worked for was already in the red. I'm solely responsible for putting them back in the black."

"Name of company?" I ask.

He laughs. "Are you interviewing me?" He leans forward, those white teeth sparkling. "Vertigo."

"Vertigo?"

He nods.

"The radio company?"

He nods again and a condescending smile pulls at his lips.

"They were in the red?" I'm surprised I hadn't heard anything about that.

"They made some bad decisions. Just like your idea to have tofu sausages."

"Excuse me?" I ask, annoyed at this entire exchange. I wish

I'd had Midge order in.

"Let's face it, your idea to do non-meat sausages isn't working. It's not driving business, it's taking time away from the business you should be focusing on." He picks up the menu to peruse it before we're finished talking about the subject.

The burn of my hives itch my neck, but I ignore it because he can't know how much I want to reach across this table and throat-punch him.

The waitress comes over, fills our water glasses and places the pitcher on the table.

"I'm Viv, do you know what you'd like?" she asks and I haven't even looked at the menu. At this point I'm not even sure I could swallow one of their meatballs sitting across from this guy.

"Hi, Viv. I'd like the meatloaf with a cup of your soup of the day." Michael hands her his menu. "A scotch with two ice cubes."

I roll my eyes right before Viv directs her attention to me. "The pot pie and vodka tonic, two limes." She takes my menu and speeds off to another table.

"Sausage sales were declining. Health-conscious people don't want to eat a heart attack in a tube. I thought it was a good way to position the company as being more health-conscious." Why am I rationalizing my decision to this man?

"Well, unfortunately for Santora Sausage it wasn't. You incurred too many costs by having to change lines and make new ones, not to mention the cost to develop the new packaging, roll out a new marketing plan. I could go on. Either way, no one wants to eat a tofu sausage made by a sausage company. People hear the word 'sausage' and no matter what's inside the skin, it doesn't scream healthy. Hey, everyone has failed at something, kudos for trying." He pulls out his phone again.

"Why did you invite me to lunch?" I can barely get the question out past the giant ball of rage lodged in my throat.

He peeks up from his phone and I swear he switched spots

with someone after we got out of the cab because he doesn't remind me of the polite man in my office.

"Truth?"

"Yes." My fingers twist the napkin.

"You're sexy and I thought we shared something the other night at your parents."

I laugh, a hollow and empty laugh. "What exactly did we share?"

"Don't play hard-to-get, Tahlia. You don't have to with me. It can be casual." He shrugs. "I heard about what happened with your fiancé, Chase Webber." His face contorts into a look that says, *Bad deal*. "A Webber, could you imagine?"

I glance out the window to calm my nerves. Who does this guy think he is? His phone rings and I roll my eyes.

"Go ahead and answer," I tell him, never looking at him.

"You want *me* to answer your phone?" he asks and when I look up, he's fiddling with his own phone again.

I dig in my purse, grabbing the call right before it goes to voicemail. I'd answer a call from the IRS right now if it meant I didn't have to continue my conversation with this man.

"Hello?" I answer and turn my sights on the street.

"Another bad dining experience?"

Lucas.

I'd recognize his voice from an echo through a long tunnel. It's deep and resonates in every cell in my body.

"Where are you?" I ask.

"Close. Is the suit business or pleasure?"

I turn around, searching the restaurant, but I don't see him. "Business."

"Good. I thought maybe you'd forgotten all about me until I saw the urge to kill in your eyes."

I search the street again, but there are so many people shuffling to return to work there's no way I'll find him unless he stands right outside the window. "Where are you?"

"One o'clock by the newsstand."

I locate the newsstand and there he is in jeans, a t-shirt and a jacket with one hand stuffed into his pocket and the other holding the phone to his ear.

"Ditch the suit and I'll take you to lunch." The smile he gives me dares me to refuse him.

I grin back and then do what I have to get out of the remainder of this lunch from hell. "Really? Oh, my God. I'll be right there!" I screech into the phone and Michael actually looks up from his phone.

"You're laying it on pretty thick there," Lucas says with a chuckle.

"No. No. I'm sure he'll understand. It can't be avoided." I continue with my lie as I stand up and retrieve my coat from behind Michael. The bastard never even gets up.

"What a gentleman you have there." Lucas continues talking in my ear and for some reason I can't hang up on him.

I sandwich the phone between my shoulder and ear, swinging my arms through my jacket and buttoning it closed.

"I'll be right there," I say in a frantic tone.

"Don't click me off yet. I want to hear what this jackass is going to say."

I hold the phone in my hand, placing my purse on my shoulder.

"Sorry, Michael, I have to go. My friend has an emergency."

"Really? You're leaving me?" He raises both his eyebrows.

"Yes, but let's get something straight. I may have jumped the gun on the tofu thing, but I still believe it's a viable option, and if my dad thinks you're doing good for the company then I won't say anything about your earlier proposition. But from now on when you're at work ignore the fact that my office exists from this point forward, got it?"

He shakes his head as though I'm a child who doesn't need his full attention. Talk about self-entitled.

I walk out of the Corridor and turn toward the newsstand, but I'm pulled into a hard chest before I can turn the corner. An instant later lips meet mine. On the corner of Van Ness and Fell, I make a public spectacle of myself as I make out with a man who either thinks I'm crazy or hot. Maybe both.

EIGHTEEN

L UCAS SLOWS OUR KISS and although I don't want it to end, there could be a zillion people who recognize me here in the business district.

"If I take you to lunch will you actually finish your meal this time?" he asks, his hands still linked behind my back, keeping me pressed to him.

"How did you get my number? How did you know I'd be here?" I ask, ignoring his question.

He chuckles. "You didn't say whether you'd go to lunch with me."

"Answer my question first." I cross my arms over my chest.

He sighs. "You should password protect your phone."

"When?" I ask, but the memory quickly comes back. "The half hour I actually slept at your apartment."

His eyebrows raise and I shake my head.

"Smooth."

"Only when it's something I really want." He pulls me into him and I let my hands drop to my sides.

"And how did you know I was here?"

He bites his lower lip and how I would love to pull that lip free. "I had an appointment down here and saw the two of you get out of the cab. I wasn't going to interrupt you, but when I saw the daggers you were shooting that guy I figured you wouldn't mind the interruption."

"You figured right." I smile.

"Good. Now, lunch?" He raises an eyebrow.

"Yes," I say and step back, my gaze dipping down to his aged Pearl Jam t-shirt.

He places his finger under my chin and brings my gaze to his, which has no more of the playful quality I like so much. Now he's serious. "We need to talk."

I nod, agreeing, because as much as I hate to admit it, I'm not the casual sex kind of girl I want to be. I like Lucas. And I'd like to know now if that's not going to work for him rather than really get my heart invested.

"There's this place down the way from here," he says. "Let's go."

His hand slides down my arm until his fingers are linked with mine. We walk down the sidewalk, dodging the oncoming people as he leads the way. Three blocks away, he opens the door to a sandwich place. Again, there's a line well past the cashier and every table is full. The anxiety that we might not be able to find somewhere to sit starts rushing forward, but I try to push it back.

"Crowded," I mention and he laughs.

"Yeah, but no worries, they seat you after you order."

I notice a guy directing people to tables as other patrons leave, and a busboy rushing around to clean off tables just as fast as he can.

"Worry more about what you're going to order. The line can go fast." Lucas points to the chalkboard menu above the cashier.

There's jargon I don't understand and it all seems so confusing.

"You order for me," I suggest.

Lucas' hand lands on the small of my back and he squeezes closer to me to allow a group of men to pass by. God, his chest feels so good.

"I'm not ordering for you, but I'll tell you what I've tried. I prefer their hot subs over their cold ones. The Italian and processed meat is the best, but they have some carving sandwiches that they're known for."

I look at him quizzically. "Gee, thanks for narrowing down my choices." My eyes focus on the menu and the line continues moving forward.

"Yeah, sorry." He shrugs, but his voice shows no sign of truly being apologetic.

"Did you notice that we're always in line somewhere together?" I say the random thought in my head. The first time I met Lucas I was in line at the boxing event, then he was at the front of the line at the horseback riding, the yacht we stood in line for drinks and to get off the boat, then the diner and now here.

He chuckles. "You're great company," he softly says, pretending to bow.

"Next!" a lady screams and Lucas' happy smile grows serious as we step up to the cashier.

"Carved turkey and avocado sandwich with the works, hot." I say my order and Lucas looks impressed that I did it correct without any questions from the cashier.

Lucas gives his Reuben order, pays for our subs, adding on chips and drinks, and then we wait in line again to be seated.

The whole process moves faster than I would have suspected and soon we're seated in a booth along the back wall with our two sandwiches, deli chips and two sodas. The anxiety of being somewhere different fades and I take the opportunity to check out the restaurant. It's decorated in red vinyl booths and old signs that say Tavern Meats and Selections. I know the company.

They've been around as long as Santora Sausage.

"Does Tavern own this place?" I ask, noticing every piece of art on the walls has their logo on them.

Lucas glances around and shrugs. "Maybe."

"Huh." I bite the inside of my cheek, contemplating if that's what Santora Sausage should have done. We supply to a bunch of different delis and restaurants around the world, but none where all their sausage comes from us exclusively.

"What?" he asks and takes a bite of his sandwich.

"Nothing." I wave him off. "Business never seems very far from my mind."

His eyes crease and he places his sandwich down.

"Can I ask you a question?" He takes his napkin and wipes his mouth.

"Sure."

"You're not a Pilates instructor, are you?"

I stare blankly at him, trying to remember why he thinks that. I rack my brain for recollection on when I ever told him what I do. Then it dawns on me. The horseback riding when I told him and Aaron that I was a Pilates instructor.

"Oh." I release my breath. "I'm not. I said that because I didn't want anyone to know where I work in case I had a stage-five clinger or something." I bite into my sandwich, which I hate to admit is awesome. I'm going to pretend it's the mayonnaise and special seasoning and not the meat that makes the sandwich mouthwatering.

"Yeah, I figured." There's something in his tone. Annoyance? "What *do* you do?"

"Um . . ." I pause because with my name comes expectations and it's not like Lucas understands yet that I'm not what my name implies. "I'm an executive at Santora Sausage . . ." He waits for me to finish, but I know he knows what I'm about to say. "My family owns the company."

"Tahlia Santora?" he says, with what I think is some disdain lacing his voice.

I set my sandwich down, my stomach unsure if it can handle eating while we're having this conversation. I don't say anything, but wait for him to speak.

"In truth, I put two and two together when we met your dipshit ex. I was going to question you at the diner, but you ran off with my cinnamon roll."

A nervous laugh escapes my throat. "I'm sorry."

"You don't have to apologize, Tahlia. I understand why you did it." The odd thing is that I believe he's not upset that I lied, but there's still something wrong.

"Well, I don't make a habit of lying."

He nods, picking up his sandwich, and that smirk returns to his lips. "I know, but we do need to talk about you taking my cinnamon roll." He winks and then bites into the sandwich, the tension around the table disappearing.

He chews, swallows and I place a chip in my mouth, testing my stomach.

"I like you. Although I appreciate the fact that you're inexperienced in the casual sex department because I'm not looking for a fuck buddy right now." He smiles, bringing his straw between those delicious lips and sucks up some soda.

"Oh," I say like a moron who can't string together two words.

"Anything you want to say?" he asks, placing his cup down and picking up his sandwich again.

"I like you, too." The way it comes out of my mouth is prim and proper and I curse myself internally.

"Gee, thanks, Mary Ellen. Can we go to the malt shop after school and share a shake?" One side of his lips ticks up.

I pick up a chip and throw it at him. It hits him square in the nose and drops down to his shirt. He plucks it up and tosses it in his mouth.

"I ran out of the diner because I thought I was just another conquest for you. Like maybe you had a system where you get girls to sleep with you and then move on. I overreacted." I look down to the table where I'm playing with the chips. "Which my friends told me, by the way."

"The one with the unicorn van?" he questions, taking another bite of his sandwich.

"Yeah, and Whitney." He nods, remembering them. "They thought I needed a rebound guy. Someone to make me forget Chase."

He finally pushes his sandwich to the side and rounds the booth over to my side, placing one arm along the top of the booth seat. His other lies on the table, blocking me in. He leans in close. "And what do you want, Tahlia?"

Shivers run up my neck and I'm thankful my hair isn't pulled into my usual ponytail today.

"I want you," I say more to my sandwich than Lucas.

I watch as his hand leaves the table and rises toward my face. He places it on my cheek and turns my head to face him.

"For another night?"

"More."

He smiles wide. "And Chase?" he asks.

"Chase who?" I answer back and his smile reaches his eyes.

"That's what I want to hear." He moves forward, placing his lips gently on mine.

I've never been in to the whole public affection thing, but with Lucas it's as though we're in our own little bubble secluded from the world.

A HALF HOUR LATER, my belly is full, my heart is warm

and Lucas walks me to the doors of Santora Sausage.

"Thanks for lunch," I say and he cages me against the glass door, his face millimeters away from mine. Not exactly appropriate behavior for a vice-president.

"You're welcome. What are your plans for tonight?"

I want to meet his family to see if they all have his gorgeous green eyes because I think I'd kidnap him and force him to marry me just to have his kids.

"Nothing I can't cancel."

"Good. I'll pick you up at seven." He leans forward, kisses my cheek and steps back. "Text me your address," he says over his shoulder as he walks away and then turns the corner out of my vision.

I fumble in my purse to reach my phone. Once it's in my hand, I text-message Whit and Lennon.

>*Me: SOS*

>*Lennon: Did you steal a cinnamon roll again?*

>*Me: I'm serious. HELP! I need a hook-up.*

>*Lennon: Tahl, they don't have those special massage places anymore.*

>*Me: Where's Whit?*

>*Lennon: Working for the man.*

>*Me: ugh, I needed Webber-type connections.*

>*Lennon: What for?*

>*Me: I need a wax and a pedicure NOW.*

>*Lennon: I know a place my friend recommended.*

Me: Where? I'll call right now.

Lennon: I'll pick you up. You at headquarters?

Me: You don't need to go with me. And headquarters? Really!?

Lennon: I need to go anyway, I have a hot date tonight.

Me: They'll be able to fit both of us?

Lennon: I'll be there in ten.

Having dealt with Lennon's crazy behavior for half my life, I know to let the topic go and just wait. Sometimes it pays to be the boss because you can do things like skip out on work for an hour to make sure you have a pretty pussy for your date later that evening. No, that's *not* in the employee handbook.

A half hour later, Lennon rolls up to the curb, completely disregarding the line of traffic she's blocking. Her old van is wrapped with a picture of a unicorn throwing up and shitting rainbows and I hold my purse in front of my face as I slide into the van, not wanting anyone who works for me to recognize me.

The second my butt hits the seat she hits the gas and I fly back into the seat.

"Jeez," I say, but she's too busy flipping another driver off to pay attention to me. "Where are we going?"

She glances over at me and smirks. I now know nothing good is going to come out of her mouth.

"It's a surprise."

"Surprises from you are never good."

She raises her hand to my face. "Just relax and enjoy the ride."

Trying to take her advice, I relax as much as I can with her barreling down the 101 going eighty while her hands rest at the bottom of the steering wheel.

We arrive outside the city to what appears to be more of an industrial area than the downtown high-end spas I'm used to.

"This is not what I was thinking," I say, not unbuckling myself.

"I know it's not posh, but believe me, you're going to love the mud bath." She undoes her seatbelt, grabs her shoulder bag and leaves me in the van.

I sit and stare at the grey building with a neon sign that reads SPA in red lettering. Flashing, I might add. Flashing as though we're on the Las Vegas Strip and it's fighting for attention. There's no one in a five-mile radius to alert of their services.

My phone buzzes in my purse and I pull it out to see a text from Lucas.

Lucas: Address? You aren't trying to ditch me, are you?

I chuckle to myself and then send him my address.

Me: I'll be ready for seven. That's if my body hasn't been chopped up in little pieces by then.

He responds right away.

Lucas: Should I send the cavalry!?

Me: It's possible. You should see the spa Lennon's dragged me to on Industrial Ave . . . let's just say the word shady doesn't cut it.

Lucas: LOL If you go missing I'll be sure to take a drive down Industrial Ave and look for the unicorn van. At least I'll be able to tell the cops your last known location.

Me: Gee thanks. Such a hero.

Lucas: Are you implying that you'd like to see me in a pair of super hero tights. I might be able to swing it. ;)

Lennon bangs on the glass window of her door and I startle

then turn to look at her.

"Come on." She's smiling as though it's every day that you go to some strange building on the outskirts of the city and spread-eagle for some stranger. I can envision it now, me unwilling to undress for Lucas because layers of skin have been ripped off me. I shake my head, gripping my purse in my hands like an old lady in a bad part of town.

"Don't be a priss, Tahl." She jogs around the front of her van, and I quickly lock my door before she can open it.

She rolls her eyes, holds up her keyset, unlocks the door and opens it before I can argue.

"I promise it will be fine," she says. Her eyes hold her 'you can trust me' look that you don't see very often. The last time I saw that look was when she told me my life would continue after Chase. In her most honest form, the true Lennon appears. The caring side, the one who would hunt down and kill anyone who hurt someone she loves.

> *Me: Gotta run. Lennon's harassing me to get going. See you tonight!*

I toss my phone back in my purse and climb out of the car. Lennon's smile grows wide, as does my own until we're walking past the glass door inside the building. Once the door rattles shut behind us, I almost run back out once I see who's waiting for us.

"WHAT ARE YOU DOING here?" I say, not moving from my spot by the door in case I need to flee.

"Should I ask you the same thing?" Whitney says, sitting in a chair next to her co-worker, Kelsey, who I've met a couple of times before.

I point to Lennon. "She brought me, what's your excuse?"

Whit glances at Lennon, who's ignoring our conversation and is checking us in with the receptionist.

Whitney and Kelsey exchange a series of serious looks and then Whitney stands and nods for me to meet her by the plant in the corner. I'm not sure why since we're the only customers in the room. We're probably the only customers today.

"We're here for a story," Whitney whispers. I'm not sure what my face must morph into but Whitney immediately pushes her hands through the air, insinuating for me to calm down. "It's not a huge thing."

"Well, you should expand if you don't want me to start hyperventilating right now," I say and she bites the inside of her cheek and glances back to Kelsey, who is stuck in a conversation with Lennon now.

"It's a story about a disgruntled employee who claims certain favors are received here."

"Favors?"

She widens her eyes.

"Okay, but . . ."

"They only hire men to service the spa customers." Whitney says each word slowly, as though I wasn't magna cum laude at Stanford and can't understand what's being implied.

I place my hands out in front of me. "Let me get this straight. Lennon brought me to a brothel before a date with Lucas?"

Whitney nods and I glance to Lennon in disgust.

"I'm not even sure she knows," Whit says and follows my vision back to Lennon and Kelsey. "I might have mentioned this place to her in passing a few months ago when we were first thinking of doing a story, but I didn't give her any details. She must have checked it out on her own."

A slow smirk forms on my face. "Well, I'm not saying anything."

"Me either." Whitney smiles and we each go back to the chairs to join the other two.

"Shouldn't you be with a bunch of hot football gods?" Lennon asks Kelsey.

Kelsey is the sports newscaster at the TV station where Whitney works and every time we see her Lennon is constantly asking her questions about the locker rooms.

"It's not football season," Kelsey says, smiling over at Whitney.

"I know it has to be some sports season. Wouldn't you rather be with naked dudes than here with a bunch of chicks?" Lennon continues to pry and the three of us laugh, Kelsey understanding Whitney has filled me in.

"Whitney and Kelsey," the lady calls them and they stand, Whitney's hand resting on my shoulder briefly before the two walk over.

"See you in there," Lennon says, grabbing a magazine and reading.

On the cover is a naked woman with a man blocking any views of her lady parts as his hands massage her. The title reads, *The Art of Sensual Massage*. I laugh and Lennon turns down the cover to look at me.

"I'm not sure how long I can read this before I'm completely turned on." She hands it over to me. "Take this with you to show boxer boy. Maybe he can get some tips."

I take the magazine from her hands and place it down on the table between us. "I think I'll let boxer boy figure me out all on his own."

She reaches over and slaps my knee. "That a girl. Your kinky side is coming out."

I remain quiet because I could never compare to Lennon and the things she's told me she does in the bedroom. Santora women weren't built to use a sex swing, or anal beads, or nipple clamps . . .

Five minutes go by and finally a guy appears from the back and calls our names. He's about our age and shirtless and if that's not a dead giveaway for what Whitney said this place is I don't know what is.

"Man service?" Lennon cocks her eyebrow my way. "Me likey."

She's quick to follow the guy down the hall. He's attractive and he knows it by the way he swaggers in front of her.

"Madam Scarlett will be right with you." He signals for me to sit in the chair and then points to Lennon. "You, follow me."

"Okay." Lennon shoots me an 'I just won the lottery' look and practically skips after him. Knowing her, she might not mind the extra benefits this spa offers if Whitney's source is correct.

Madam Scarlett is actually a fifty-five-year-old woman with candles on every possible surface of her room, but she does a bang-up job on my bikini wax. She barely hurt me and I feel a little guilty for judging way too fast based on outward appearance.

After Madam Scarlett's painless wax job, I'm taken to Madam Alexandra for a mani-pedi. I'm trying not to be offended that I haven't had a man's hands on me this entire time and wonder if there's a camera somewhere where the men all vote on who gets who and no one's choosing me.

Madam Alexandra is younger, probably in her early twenties and very enthusiastic about her job. After my nails have set, she approaches me. "Your friend Lennon has purchased a massage for you. If you'll follow me." She slowly saunters down the hall, seemingly in no rush, while I scramble to find a clock that will tell me what time it is. Madam Scarlett had me disrobe and lock all my belongings in a locker, including my phone. She didn't seem like someone you argue with, so I abided.

"Um. I don't need a massage," I say to Madam Alexandra's back, but she shakes her head and keeps walking.

"She said you might be shy, but she insisted." She never even glances back at me.

"She's persistent, I know, but I really don't have time. I have another engagement."

She stops at a door labeled 'Tantric number five.' Her hand rests on the doorknob as the word 'tantric' flashes red in my head like their neon sign outside.

"Really, I'm fine. I'd like to go." I take a step back, clutching my robe in front of me.

She opens the door. "I promise, Miss Santora, it's a very relaxing experience."

I stay on the outside of the door, peering through to find it similar to any massage place—a table in the middle, low light, warm air. I'm not sure if I was expecting ropes suspended from the ceiling or maybe a wall of crops or what, but there's no toys, no fetish stuff, so maybe my mind is in overdrive.

"Just a massage?" I clarify and her face remains cold stone, no smile like she's had with me the entire time she was working on my nails.

"Just oil and hands, Miss Santora," she clarifies and, trusting a woman I met only an hour ago, I step forward into the room.

She shuts the door immediately and I scope out the room, until I find a note on a table that asks for me to disrobe and lie on my stomach. Not any different than every other massage I've had since I was fifteen.

I take off my robe, hang it up, and lie on the table, positioning the sheet over my backside, and wait.

I should get up.

What am I doing?

What if I get a man?

I'm just about to get off the table when the door to the side opens and I hear footsteps enter the room. Soft music starts playing and the scent of jasmine fills the room.

I'm afraid to look and since I'm not sure if it's a male or female, I lie there stiff as a mannequin.

"Calm," a male says with a voice so low I barely register it. His oily hands land on my thighs and run along my muscles, soothing and relaxing them.

He explores my body with a professionalism and politeness that's expected from a masseuse and my eyes drift shut. I'm thanking Lennon for being the persistent nag she is and buying me a massage, and shaming Whitney for thinking the worst of this place. I relax into the experience and put my issues and fears aside while the man pulls and tugs on each of my toes.

Heaven. This man's hands are heaven. A little rough, but I've never had a male masseur before because I've always been fearful of feeling uncomfortable that his hands might venture into the no-no zones.

Every muscle slowly loses its usual tension and I want to get this man's name and come here every day. I'm close to drifting off when his two hands slide up under my towel and grab each of my ass cheeks.

"Hey!" I flip over and two green eyes reminiscent of grass in the middle of spring stare back at me. "Lucas?"

He holds his hands up in the air, a devilish smile on his lips. "I didn't think you'd mind since I've already been thoroughly acquainted with that part of your anatomy."

I grip the two-by-two towel, trying to cover both my breasts and my vagina. Not happening.

He steps forward and slowly loosens each of my fingers until the towel drops to my lap. His eyes lock with mine with a promise of much more than a massage. I want to lock my legs around his waist and feel him push inside of me. If only the fear of someone walking in didn't occupy my mind.

"What are you doing here?" I ask, allowing him to lean toward me and press his soft lips to my collarbone.

"Exactly what I said I was going to do. I drove down Industrial Avenue. Your friend's van isn't exactly subtle."

He licks up the side of my neck until he sucks my earlobe into his mouth. God, this man makes the rest of the world fade away.

"That doesn't explain how you got into this room," I say with blatant need in my voice.

He places his body weight on me, so I lean back on the table. "I slipped the girl at the front a hundred-dollar bill, and here I am," he says and for some reason I ask no more questions. Maybe it's the distraction of his lips, or the pressing of his erection between my legs over the roughness of his jeans.

He picks his head up, peering into my eyes once again. "The

thought of you at a spa—naked, with someone else's hands on you . . . I hope it's okay." Then his head disappears between my breasts, while his hands knead each one. I nod as his tongue swirls around my nipple before his attention switches to the other and then back again without favoring either one.

I swear I grow even wetter with the thought that he wanted no other man to touch me.

His lips trail down my stomach with open kisses and he stops right before my newly waxed mound and looks up at me through his long eyelashes.

"I've missed the taste of you," he says, licking his lips.

"It hasn't been that long."

He grips my ass and hoists my hips off the table to reach his mouth. "Too long," he mutters. With gentle swirls of his tongue, he teases me until I can't hold back the moans that so desperately want to escape. Right as I'm teetering on the cliff, he lets my hips fall to the table and guides my hand between my legs.

"I want to watch you while I undress."

A flash of apprehension runs through me, but I push it away and begin massaging my clit. Now is no time to worry about what someone might think if they knew I'd masturbated in front of a man.

Between my legs, I watch him shrug off his t-shirt, then undo the button of his jeans until they slide down his legs. Lastly, his thumbs push each side of his boxer briefs down his legs and his perfect cock springs free. My mouth waters. I understand him wanting to taste me because there's nothing I want more than to have his dick in my mouth.

Stepping forward between my legs, he moves his cock up and down my pussy, coating wetness onto his rigid length. I move my hand down to wrap around him and a groan escapes his throat when my thumb rubs along the tip.

I sit up, unable to go any longer without his mouth on

mine. He beats me to it and smashes our lips together, his tongue exploring my mouth, then my jaw, and my ear. My head falls back, granting him access to any inch of skin he demands. He nibbles on my nipple and forcefully pulls me to the edge of the table. My hands, searching for something to grasp, feel a foil packet next to my thigh. I grab it and rip it open.

Lucas steps back and juts out his hips. He doesn't have to ask because I'm already rolling the condom down his hardness.

His hands mold to my hips as I guide him into me. *Pure bliss.* He fills my pussy and pulls back immediately, taking charge and hammering my hips back and forth, me meeting him thrust for thrust.

I don't have to tell Lucas I want it harder, he figures it out on his own by the sounds escaping me. The exotic scent of the jasmine only spurs my want for him. He tells me how hot I am, how he's hard for me all the time, how he has to beat off to the memory of fucking me every day. Every muscle in my body tightens and all my nerve endings are tingling when Lucas places his thumb on my engorged clit and begins rubbing. I come and a tidal wave of ecstasy rolls over me, my fingers digging into his shoulders and my legs clamped around his waist.

Without stopping, he continues to praise my body and pound into me, joining me moments later, a flush to his cheeks and my taste on his lips.

"I wonder how much Lennon's going to have to pay for that massage?" I unhook my legs from his waist as he falls on top of my sweaty torso.

He chuckles. "I should be paying you," he says, delivering one kiss between my breasts. "Hopefully tonight I can keep it in my pants a little longer."

He stands back up and I follow, sitting up and not trying to use the small towel to hide myself this time. Walking to the trashcan, he disposes the condom.

"What did you think would happen here?" I ask, curious.

Bending down, he picks up his pants and pulls them up over his legs. "I thought I'd mess with you a little. But I swear I thought you'd have a sheet over you and I for sure thought you'd have your underwear on." He raises a brow and closes the button of his jeans.

"Usually they do place a warm sheet or towel over the top of me," I say, eyeing the stack of white linens in the corner.

"Good thing I snuck in then. I don't want anyone else having the pleasure of seeing all you have to offer." He grins and puts his t-shirt back on and I miss his naked chest already.

"No one can please me like you can, Mr. Cummings." I bat my eyelashes and he steps forward again, easing my legs apart with his palms.

"You got that right." He plants a small kiss on my lips. "Your friends are probably waiting, wondering what held you up." He kisses me again, not lingering too long. "I'll pick you up tonight at seven." His lips meet mine a third time and then he's gone, out the side door way too quick for my liking.

Ten minutes later, I'm back in my suit with my cell phone in hand listening to a message from Lucas asking if I was at the spa. I hit save on the message because I like the idea of being able to hear his voice whenever I want, and walk out of the hallway to find the three girls waiting for me.

"Hot damn, you're flushed," Lennon says, pointing to my face.

I shake my head, trying not to smile.

"I thought my source was full of shit. Maybe not," Whitney adds, giving me the once-over.

"Or it could be that I just saw boxer boy sneak out the side door and get into his truck in the parking lot." Lennon smirks.

"You and your damn unicorn van," I say, passing all of them to get outside for some fresh air.

"I think you mean damn boxer boy and his unicorn cock." Whitney laughs and follows me out.

THE SUN IS LOW in the sky, darkening my bedroom with its shadow. I stand in front of my mirror to double-check my make-up, my hair and my outfit. Surely, a nice dress with flats won't be overdressed nor underdressed. I should've asked him where we were going this afternoon, but I was a little . . . preoccupied.

I pick up my brush to put a little more blush on, then realize I'm still so flushed thinking about this afternoon, there's no need for it.

Questions flood my head on what exactly I'm doing with Lucas, but I push them away because I'm enjoying my time with him and I don't want to psychoanalyze us. Before my thoughts can venture too much into the minefield that is my brain, my phone rings.

The doorman of my building notifies me that Lucas is here and I let him know he's okay to come up. I don't require a call for regular visitors like Whitney and Lennon, but anyone else requires my permission.

I take the deepest breath I can and walk out of my bedroom

to wait and a couple minutes later there's a knock on my door.

My flats pad along the hardwood floors and when I reach my front door I open it to find Lucas standing there in a suit. I now know where the term suit porn comes from. Inwardly, I cringe at my more casual attire.

"I should change," I say, ready to spin around and head back to my bedroom.

He grabs my wrist, halting my movements, and steps into my apartment. "No, you shouldn't."

"But you're in a suit." I motion with my hand to the perfection that is Lucas in a fitted suit.

He looks down at himself as though he forgot. "I am."

I hate that I automatically assumed he wouldn't take me anywhere too dressy because he's not used to having a silver spoon in his mouth. I contemplate how I would've dressed if Chase or Michael were picking me up.

"Really, I'd like to change," I protest, but he's already shaking his head.

He shrugs out of his jacket, walks down my hall and places it on the back of my breakfast stool.

"Let's go." He passes by me and once he reaches the door, he turns on his heels and holds out his hand.

"But—"

Again, a shake of his head tells me to stop fighting, I'm not going to win this one. I grab my purse from the foyer table and meet him at the door. He waits for me to lock up before he links his hand with mine and we walk down the hallway toward the elevator.

"Was that your slick way of having to come back to my apartment?" I ask as we wait by the elevator, still in silence.

He tips his head my way. "I don't think I needed to leave my jacket for you to ask me in after we finish our date, did I?"

I giggle, unable to hide the fact he's right. I'll probably be dragging him into my apartment by his tie after we eat.

The elevator arrives, and I step in first. I watch his finger press the lobby button and remember that finger inside of me, arching until it hit my G-spot. My body floods with warmth as a vision of the two of us this afternoon comes to mind.

"You look beautiful," he leans over and whispers in my ear.

I glance over, finding his signature smirk on his face, the one that promises I'll be squirming under him again in a few hours. "Thank you. You look very handsome." His cheeks pink slightly before the elevator doors ding open and he distracts himself by holding the doors for me.

I step through, nodding to my fellow elderly residents walking in. Lucas stays and holds the doors open until they're through and then releases his arm. Again, his hand finds mine and we walk out into the street.

It's a perfect spring night with warm air surrounding us and my mood feels light, like anything is possible. I realize for the first time in a long time that what I feel is contentment, peace.

"I thought we'd cab it," he says and turns to my doorman to call a taxi.

I don't even have to answer because in seconds, I'm already tucked into the back of the cab and Lucas is rambling off an address that I can't place.

"Where are we going?" I ask, crossing my legs and facing him.

"I called in a few connections and got us into a speakeasy." He lowers his voice. "It's a quiet lounge. We'll have dinner and drinks and then I thought we'd maybe go for a walk on the pier."

"Sounds amazing," I answer, wondering what kind of connections he has to get us into a speakeasy. He must know people in high places.

The cab parks along the curb and we each climb out, Lucas paying the cab driver through the passenger window. I look around while I'm waiting and see there's a line of restaurants down either side of the road and I wonder which one houses the speakeasy.

Lucas approaches me, links his hand with mine and leads us down the street.

"You're surprised?" he asks.

"That you know of a speakeasy?" I clarify, delaying my answer a beat. He nods. "A little. They're hard to find."

He nods a few more times, a smile playing on his lips. "That they are."

Thankfully, he doesn't appear to be upset that I wouldn't think he'd have the connections to gain us access to a speakeasy. But I don't think it's that I'm surprised, as much as I like him not having those things. I would have been more than ecstatic to have him take me to a movie, or bowling, or whatever fun activities he enjoys and not a five-star restaurant. How different he is from my usual type of guy is part of what I'm attracted to. The fact he's comfortable in his own skin and doesn't feel the need to impress anyone.

We enter the restaurant, but he informs the waitress that we're actually there for the Vector and she nods, turning her back on us and walking away. Lucas motions for me to follow and we walk through the tables and down a set of stairs.

Lucas slides past me as the hostess walks away and he enters a code into the keypad. It opens and we're left in a four-by-four room with another door in front of us. Lucas knocks and a giant of a man pushes the door open from the other side. He smiles, holding his hand out to Lucas.

"Lucas, feels like it's been forever." The burly guy smiles through his curly beard.

"How are you, Benny?" They do the guy handshake-hug thing and then Lucas' hand comes to rest on the small of my back.

"This is Tahlia," he introduces me and I hold my hand out to

Benny and his entire hand swallows up my own when we shake.

"Very nice to meet you. If you got Lucas to actually bring you here for *dinner*, you must be some woman." He grins at Lucas and when I glance back, Lucas is rolling his eyes.

The three of us quiet for a moment and Lucas' back stiffens when another man rounds the bar.

"Let's go find a seat," he says to me and Benny glances at the older gentleman and shoots Lucas an almost sympathetic smile, the kind that would suggest he's apologizing for something.

"Enjoy, you two," he says, and heads over to the bar.

Lucas leads us to a small table and pulls out my chair for me like a gentleman. He relaxes into his own chair and I take the opportunity to check out the hidden lounge.

The lights are dimmed with a softness that casts a rose-colored glow over everything in the room. The lounge chairs are red velvet and the cushions on the wood chairs are covered with the same material. The room is intimate and the low ceiling makes it cozy.

"I love it," I tell him when my eyes land back on him.

His eyes are fixated on mine as he leans back in his chair, one leg resting on the knee of the other. There's a casualness about him that says he's comfortable here.

"Me too," he says and a twinge of excitement rushes through my veins.

Our eyes lock together as we sit in silence, just the hum of the handful of other patrons scattered throughout the room between us.

I break the connection first and glance down at the table. "So, do we get menus?" I ask, crossing my legs to stop the tingling between my thighs.

"We do." He raises his hand and a guy walks over. I wonder how long he was waiting since he has water glasses and menus in hand for us.

"Thank you," I say and the man looks from Lucas to me and back, eyes wide as saucers. I'm confused by this whole experience. The young kid scurries away and Lucas examines the small piece of paper in his hand.

"Do you know other people here?" I whisper over the table and Lucas peers up.

"No, not really." He focuses back down.

"That kid looked scared," I say.

He looks over my shoulder where I imagine the kid is and then back to me. He shrugs his shoulders.

Figuring this topic of conversation is dead, I study my menu and decide that the scallops sound amazing.

"Just so you know, you can't get these dishes in the main dining room. It's strictly for Vector."

"Oh, really?" I smile. I place the menu down on the table. "I'm going to have the scallops with risotto."

Lucas places his menu down too, "Sounds great, but I need red meat so I'm going with the medallions."

"That sounds yummy, too."

The waiter comes over, takes our orders and we sit there a little longer in silence. Although Lucas seems comfortable here, he's also a bit on edge, checking the door every time he hears Benny's voice. There's something off about tonight, but I have no idea what.

"Have you been here before?" I initiate the conversation.

"Yeah. Long time ago, though. Benny and I have been friends since grade school."

I smile at him, happy that he's offering more information about himself than I asked for. "Oh, that's awesome. Whitney and Lennon and I have been friends since childhood."

He smiles. "I guess the three of you are as different as Benny and I?"

"How so?" I ask and he freezes for a moment.

"Well, I don't see you driving a unicorn shitting a rainbow around town."

I laugh. "Very true. But how are you and Benny different?"

He straightens his back, his fingers tightly woven together on top of the table.

"Benny likes this scene. Me, not so much," he says and I look around to the secluded secret club. Then it dawns on me, it's elite. Lucas doesn't do elite.

"So why did you bring me?" I can't help but ask the question that's been burning inside of me since he told me what his plan for us was.

He studies me for a second. "Well, to be honest, I assumed this is what you're used to."

I clear my throat and cock my head to the side. "So you didn't really want to bring me here?"

He shrugs. "I don't mind bringing you here. I wanted you to be comfortable."

"At the expense of you being uncomfortable?"

"I'm comfortable."

"Then why do you keep checking the door?" I ask, taking a sip of my water.

"I figure your jackass ex might show up."

He diverts his gaze midsentence telling me that he's lying, but I don't want our date to end up in a fight so I let the observation go.

"Why don't we leave here and you can take me where *you* wanted to take me?" I grab my purse from my side and slide out my chair.

"We'll eat and then I'll take you where I would have."

I slide the chair back in but that's only so I can lean in closer to him.

"Lucas, I really like you. I don't want the five-star restaurants, the operas, the connections. I just want you. I'm excited for you to show me what you would've planned for us if I wasn't Tahlia Santora. It's exactly the reason I didn't want you to know who I was."

He looks at me long and hard. I can see the wheels turning in his head, but I have no idea what he's thinking. Without a word he pulls out his wallet, tosses bills on the table, stands and holds out his hand for me.

"Then let's go to the pier," he says.

"I'd love to."

He takes my hand and leads me out of the exclusive club and I'm happy I'm going to get to know the real him, not who he thinks I want him to be.

TWENTY-ONE

HOURS LATER, WE'RE IN a cab on the way home, my stomach stuffed full of corn dogs, nachos and pretzels. There was no white wine from the reserved collection, but cherry cola slushes instead. We rode the carousel and I leaned on his chest as we watched the street performers, the warmth of his hand holding mine as we navigated our way through the many people down by the water.

"Look at the size of the head he gave me. It's huge," Lucas says, staring down at the caricature we had done.

"He's supposed to accentuate your features. Maybe he was able to tell the size of your ego," I say with a laugh.

He grabs the drawing from my hands and looks down at it. "He didn't extenuate any of your features. You look just as beautiful."

I grab it back, making sure he knows it's mine. "I'm going to ignore the fact you think my lips are that big."

He swivels in his seat to face me. "I like your big lips." Attempting to hide his laugh, he purses his lips.

"Really? Well, then I'm not arguing about your forehead,"

I say, turning my back on him to stare out the window.

His breath tickles my neck a second later, his hand wrapping around my waist.

"I'm sorry, baby, you don't have big lips. However, if you did, I know where they'd benefit you," he whispers and I eye the cab driver who is talking on his Bluetooth.

I turn to him and his lips cover mine in a passionate kiss that sets every nerve in my body on alert for more. My hand weaves through his hair as he presses my back to the vinyl seat. His hand slides down the side of my dress to my hemline, but I grip his hand with mine, effectively stopping our kiss. Lucas' lips vibrate along mine because he's chuckling.

"No?" he questions and I shake my head to say, *No way are we doing a repeat of the night we took a cab after being on the yacht.*

"Not tonight."

He retracts his hand and slides to his own side of the cab.

"Why are you moving all the way over there?" I ask, my eyebrows raised.

"When I'm around you, I can't control myself." He holds his hands up in the air, clasps them together and places them in his lap. "They'll stay here until we get out of the cab."

"And then?"

"Now if I told you, what fun would be that be?"

"Hint?"

His gaze locks with mine, lust and desire swimming in the depth of his green hues. "No way am I spoiling the surprise." He winks and my pussy clenches.

The cab stops along the curb of my condo building and I'm already collecting my purse, preparing to slide out. Lucas stays seated, blocking my way out of the cab.

"Are you in a rush, Miss Santora?" he asks, digging out his wallet and handing money to the driver. We're both well aware that every other time I've ridden a cab with him, he's paid through the passenger window.

"Come on," I urge him, my hip knocking his, but his lips turn up. He glances to me and then back to the driver.

"Just give me a five back," he directs the cab driver.

I huff.

He laughs.

"Lucas." I roll my eyes.

He laughs again.

"Miss Santora, why are you in such a hurry?"

The cab driver is paid up and still he sits in place, his face straight as he asks me the question.

"Keep it up and I'll be keeping your suit jacket." I cross my arms over my chest and raise my eyebrows like I'm serious.

He laughs, shakes his head and climbs out of the cab.

I graciously accept his extended hand and I'm not even out of the cab before the driver speeds off, probably upset that we wasted his time with our game.

"Is this where I'm supposed to ask you in for a cup of coffee?" I ask, slowly walking to my door.

"You could ask me for a fuck and I'd gladly oblige."

A flush rushes up my neck. "So, no to the coffee then?"

The doorman opens the door for us and Lucas tips him.

"In the morning maybe?" Lucas questions as we step into the elevator.

"Are you going to expect breakfast as well?"

He looks up to the ceiling. "You do owe me a cinnamon roll." He shrugs, acting as though we're business colleagues.

"True. Will Pillsbury do?"

The elevator stops on my floor and we file out, venturing down my hallway.

He scoffs, "You stole a homemade, gooey, delicious, cinnamon roll soaked with icing and you think that a pop-open-a-tube, smack-it-on-a-cookie-sheet cinnamon roll will be a suitable replacement? No, no, Miss Santora, that will not do."

We reach my condo and his hand molds to my hip, turning me into him as he pushes me against the door. His two arms cage me in, his lips softly brush mine.

"But, Mr. Cummings, I don't know how to make a homemade cinnamon roll," I say in my high-pitched what-will-I-do voice.

His lips betray his attempt at being serious as they turn up. "I guess you'll have to let me eat something else in order to pay me back."

I look up to his face, pull his tie to break the remaining distance and crash my lips to his. Urgent and demanding, our tongues explore each other and his kiss makes it hard for my legs to support me. Our lips pull apart and I'm practically panting, locking my thighs together.

"Miss Santora, you're so forward," he says, but I push him back, dig into my purse for my key and unlock the door.

He's still standing in the hall as I back up a step into my condo. I toe out of my shoes, one at a time, leaving them in a path as I continue walking backward, then reach to my side and unzip my dress, sliding my arms out and allowing it to fall to the floor.

"Is this too forward?" I ask him.

He grips either side of my door frame, his eyes bugging out of his head. Lucas steps forward, shutting the door behind him without breaking my stare. "Never," he says, stepping toward me as he loosens his tie. The tie falls to the floor while he toes out of his loafers. He manipulates the buttons of his shirt one at a time until he stops right in front of me.

I can't keep my hands off him, so I slide them over his shoulders to push the shirt off his chest. He digs into his pockets, leaving keys, a wallet and a tube of Chap Stick on my breakfast bar.

"Allow me," I tell him, falling to my knees.

He sucks in a breath and those hard ridges on his stomach flex as I stare at him the entire time I work on unbuckling his belt, unbuttoning his pants and lastly guiding the zipper over the engorged bulge. I lick my lips as I push down his slacks and boxer briefs in one quick motion.

His perfect cock stands to attention in front of my face with a drop of pre-cum ready to drip down. My right hand grips his dick and I lick the drop from his tip.

He groans.

I become wetter.

Nothing is more of a turn-on than when you encase your entire mouth over a guy's dick and he's harder than you thought possible. Nothing is more of a turn-on than when his fingers thread through your hair and grip the strands so tight, it hurts. Nothing is more of a turn-on than when he grinds his hips because you're just that good.

Lucas does all of those things as I hollow my cheeks out and guide my mouth as far down on his cock as I can go. He's too big for me to fit the entire thing in my mouth so I fist the bottom and pump him with my hand. Every time I draw back I swirl my tongue along the sensitive underside of his mushroom tip and every time he lets out a deep, guttural groan. Seconds before I'm sure he's going to explode in my mouth, he rips me away from him. By my hair, I might add, and it makes me so wet that my panties are soaked.

I stare up at him, still on my knees, wondering why he stopped me.

"Not tonight," he murmurs, reaching under my arms and pulling me up.

Man, I love how strong he is.

He carries me into the bedroom, depositing me on the bed. I move my arms behind my back to undo my bra.

"No. I'll do it." His voice is gravelly and demanding and it solidifies that he'll be stripping soaked panties from my body.

"I thought I was taking charge tonight?" I joke as he crawls up the mattress on his hands and knees toward me.

"One night, I'll let you tie me up and whip me." He chuckles, but I'm not sure if he's serious.

I don't mind playing this cat-and-mouse game, but whips, crops or whatever else might be a little out of my league. For now, anyway.

While my mind runs through a mental arsenal of kinky sex toys, Lucas' mouth continues a path up my body. One brush of his tongue on my hot skin and I'm back in the moment with him.

His callused hands run along my skin and the wetness of his mouth follows closely behind. His fingers hook either side of my panties and he drags them down my legs. After tossing them on the ground, he hovers over me, his eyes staring into mine. The lust that's usually there is still present, but there's also the promise of more.

The weight of his body gradually falls on top of me and he cradles my face with his hands. Emotions hot and wild and somehow just as calm and reassuring swell between us. Just when I feel a pricking behind my eyes, his lips meet mine and our mouths move in a slow dance. Our tongues glide, his thumbs caress my cheeks and his length circles my center. The take-charge Lucas turns into a sweet, gentle man and I like this side of him just as much as the former.

Our hands explore each other, discovering the places on our bodies that make the other moan or whimper—for him, my hands running down his back, for me, the hollow of my neck. He never lingers too long, continuing his path of discovery to what pulls the pleasure from my lips. The wetness of his tongue circles my nipples, the hotness of his mouth sucks my pebbled nub into his mouth.

His hands fit perfectly along my hips as he turns me over

onto my stomach and slides up my body until his cock nestles between my legs. His breath tickles my ear and all too soon his cock leaves my skin because his lips are sucking a trail up and down my spine. He glides his hands up my arm, his fingers webbing with mine above my head while he moves back up my body.

"You're so beautiful. Your skin . . . so soft," he whispers and I turn my head to give him access to my ear. He takes the hint, nibbling on my earlobe. "I could touch you all day long and never have enough," he continues whispering while shivers rush up the back of my hairline.

I try to raise my hips to meet his own, needing more of him. Needing him inside me.

"You want me?" he asks, his fingers tightening in mine.

"Yes," I say softly into my pillow.

"I can't hear you, baby." He circles his hard length and it presses into me at just the right spot when he grinds.

"Yes!" I whimper.

His fingers dig into my skin and he turns me so I'm on my back again. He stands and reaches into his pocket to retrieve a condom and shuffles out of his already open pants and boxer briefs. His socks quickly come off and he rips open the foil packet and joins me back on the bed.

I rest my weight on my elbows, watching him glide the latex down his length, and my legs open wider with the undying need to have him inside me.

He positions himself over the top of me and glides himself in, resting his weight on his elbows. Instead of rushed thrusts, he circles and grinds his hips in a slow, sensual rhythm. He sprinkles kisses all over my face, licking up my neck. My fingers run up and down his bare back. I wrap my legs up and around his waist, my heels digging into his ass.

His slow and steady thrusts spur on a building need inside of me until I can't take it anymore—I need hard and fast. My fingers dig into the flesh of his shoulder blades, my moans grow louder. He growls into my neck, speeding up the pace.

At some point in the mixture of tongues colliding, hands gripping, and moans escaping, Lucas spurs my nerves into a frenzy of excitement until I can't hold it in anymore and I unravel in his hold with his mouth swallowing down my screams.

He grinds into me a few more times and then stills, his sweaty body collapsing on top of me. Instead of withdrawing, he cages my head within his arms and kisses me until his erection wanes. Then he disappears into my bathroom.

I lie on top of the sheets trying to make sense of what just happened between us. It was different than all the other times we've been together, weighted with something more than blind passion demanding to be sated. I feel as though Lucas just made love to me, but that's crazy. We've only known each other for weeks and most of the time I was acting like a lunatic.

I have no time to mull it over because Lucas climbs on my bed, under the sheet and comforter, patting the spot next to him.

"Feel free to make yourself at home," I joke and he only smiles as if to say, *That ship sailed weeks ago.*

"Your bed is much more comfortable than mine," he says while I climb under the covers with him. His hand finds my bare hip, pulling me a little closer.

"Well, I am a princess," I joke again and that smile I adore graces his lips.

"And deserve to be treated as such." He leans over and places a chaste kiss on my temple.

I close my eyes briefly at the feeling of comfort his kiss provokes. When I open my eyes, we sit there, each resting our head in our hands, staring at one another.

"Tell me about you," he says, rubbing up and down my hip.

"You know everything. I was engaged and now I'm not. I work at my family's sausage company."

"No. That's what you do, not who you are. Did you grow up wanting to be a sausage distributor?"

"Are you trying not to laugh when you say that?"

A peal of laughter belts out of him and his head falls on my pillow. "I'm sorry. I'm sure you get it all the time."

"All. The. Time." I smile. He sits back up, pursing his lips to stay serious, trying to keep a straight face. "I grew up wanting to be Mary Fiore."

"Is that Guy Fiore's wife?"

I stare blankly at him. "Yes, Lucas, I wanted to be the wife of one of the Food Network chefs. You got me."

He chuckles again and the deep-throated sound brings me comfort. "Sorry. Who is Mary Fiore?"

"You don't know?" I ask, while flinging the covers off the bed and running into my family room to grab my basket of romantic comedies.

"Oh, boy, you are a romantic." He's not asking a question, but rather confirming something he seemed to already know for himself. "Have you never heard of Netflix?"

I look up from scouring my titles to find *The Wedding Planner*. "Of course I have, but true romance only happens in the movies."

I rush through the DVDs and when I find it, I hold it up in the air. Lucas' eyebrows rise in question.

My shoulders falter a bit at his expression. "What?"

"He sure did a number on you," he says, his eyes full of sympathy. "Tell me Tahlia, did he ever watch any of these with you?"

I stare down at my white comforter, picking off a small piece of lint and rolling it around between my finger and thumb. "What kind of man wants to watch romantic comedies?" I tried to get Chase to watch my favorite movies with me numerous times—even just *Love Actually* during the holidays—but getting

Chase to do something he didn't want to was like trying to move a skittish elephant.

"This one does."

The tingling in my nose signals I could cry at the moment, but I push it back as the apples of my cheeks rise to limits I'm not sure they've ever seen.

"Really?" I ask.

"Yes. Put it in." He slides up so his back hits the headboard, getting comfortable.

I jump up and down on my knees. "Seriously?" I clarify again.

"Tahl," he sighs and I'm not sure if it's him using my nickname or if it's the fact he's interested in sharing something I love with me, but a small piece of my splintered heart opens for this man who's become the exact opposite of who I thought he was.

"SO, YOU WANT TO become a wedding planner and fall in love with the groom?" Lucas asks, dipping his spoon into my carton of Fudge Overload ice cream.

I push my spoon into his Chunky Monkey, pulling up a heaping spoonful. "Well, the wedding planner, yes. The groom thing and my father setting me up with an Italian guy, no."

The credits continue to roll as we dig into each other's ice cream.

"Good, because I was torn on which would be easier, finding a fake fiancé or learning Italian and moving in with your parents." He laughs and I slide closer to him.

He hands me his carton and I hand him mine.

"Why aren't you a wedding planner?" he asks. My spoon slides around the cool ice cream, not actually spooning it. "If you'd rather not—"

"No. It's fine." I skim a small amount of ice cream onto my spoon. "Family obligations. I'm the oldest and there's only my younger sister. With no boys, the company's future falls on me."

He nods. "Tough gig," he says and places his ice cream on

the nightstand.

"It's not so bad. He pays me well and my dad made me work my way up so I know the business inside out."

"Hmm . . . so you're a glass-half-full girl then?" he asks, getting out of bed and putting his boxers on.

I follow him, placing my ice cream on my nightstand and throwing on a camisole and shorts. "Nothing can change, so I try the optimistic approach."

We both pick up our cartons of ice cream and walk into the kitchen.

"You could quit."

I huff. "Yeah, not an option."

I grab the carton of ice cream from him and he takes my spoon. I go to the freezer while he rinses off the spoons and places them on the other side of the sink.

"Why?" he asks and moves to the fridge. "Do you mind if I grab a water?"

"Help yourself to whatever." I climb on top of the kitchen counter, crossing my legs. "I can't leave my family in the lurch. It's really that simple."

He leans against the counter across from me, crossing his ankles, and cracks open the water bottle.

"You really are rare," he says, nodding his head a few times as his eyes bore into mine.

"What about you? Why boxing?"

His lips turn into a smile as big as a girl whose boyfriend just got down on bended knee. Or a boy whose girlfriend just got on her knees.

"I love it. It's really that simple." He laughs lightly and pushes himself off the counter to come stand in front of me.

"Since when?"

"*Rocky.*" He winks.

I laugh at the fact he uses the movie title. "Hmm . . ."

His hands skim up my bare legs, coming to rest on my pajama shorts. "What?"

"I'm trying to see Mary Fiore and Rocky Balboa as a couple." My face scrunches up and I shake my head.

"I won't be a pediatrician like the guy in the movie, but my boxing days are numbered." His hands continue gliding along my skin and I unwind my legs to spread them open. He grips my ass and slides me forward.

"Why?"

He looks up at me. "I'm getting old and my body won't be able to do it forever. The gym is my plan B."

"You're not old."

"I am in boxing. Not to mention I started late, after college, so I'll probably be hanging up my gloves soon."

I place my hands on his cheeks, and my lips turn pouty. "Are you sad?"

He smiles. "Yes and no. I knew it was going to end one day, but the gym will fill the void."

"What about your family?" I change the course of our conversation to what I hope is a happier subject.

His lips dip into a frown. "I'm not really close with them." Lucas hoists me in his arms. "Let's go watch another movie." He carries me into the bedroom like I weigh no more than a feather.

"You choose." I hurry and get under the covers, excited by the prospect of more snuggle time with him.

His fingers run across my DVDs until a Cheshire-like grin crosses his lips and he selects one. "This one." He holds up *Grease*.

"*Grease*?" I ask. He opens up the case, and takes over setting up the movie as though he's in his own home.

"I always love a story where the good girl falls in love with the bad boy." He grins over his shoulder and my perma-smile indents further into my face.

THE LIGHT STREAMS INTO my bedroom and my hand travels down his hard ridged body. Peace flows through my veins that he's here, in my bed.

My head rubs along his chest and I peek a look at his stubbled jaw as I tip my head up. I'm surprised to find him looking down at me.

"Good morning," he says, no morning grogginess in his voice.

"Morning." My own voice is a little hoarse, probably from screaming his name over and over again last night.

I pick up my head and rest my chin on his chest. "How long have you been up?"

He continues to assess me. "A while."

I squirm to get up, but he pushes me back down. "You should have woken me."

"No, I was enjoying you drooling on my chest."

I glance down to where I just was and sure enough, there's a puddle of my saliva. My face heats and I wonder if my face resembles the tomatoes my parents' housekeeper uses for that spaghetti sauce I love so much.

"I think I'll just die right now, thanks." I slide under the covers and hide.

He massages my back over the comforter. "Hey, I might as well get used to it."

I peek my head out from the covers at his admission that we'll be doing this again.

"And I guess I need to invest in earplugs."

He cocks his head, taking him a second to figure out my reference. "I don't snore," he argues and I widen my eyes. "I do?" he questions as though he's never heard that before. He slides down, taking the edge of the comforter and flipping it over our heads, tenting us inside. "I guess you will be getting used to that, then." He takes me in his strong arms and my leg wraps around his.

"Promise?" I ask.

He winks. "Promise."

Just like that, another piece of my heart belongs to him.

TWENTY-THREE

A WEEK LATER AND Lucas has spent most of those nights at my condo. The adventure date was canceled on Saturday because of overbooking so sadly I still haven't whitewater-rafted. Next weekend we're ziplining and it's Lucas' last event to host and my last event to attend per the package the girls purchased. Perfect timing if you ask me.

Lennon, Whitney and Cole are waiting for me at the table with Derek, Sammie and Todd when I finally arrive at the boxing event. This is the first time I'll see Lucas box as his girlfriend and to be honest, I'm more nauseous this time than the first time around. Regardless, no matter how much anxiety I have, no Everclear will pass these lips.

Lennon bounces back and forth on her feet, pretending she's punching me. "You ready to see your man?" she asks me and I roll my eyes, hugging Whitney and Cole hello.

"Where is he?" Whitney asks, peering around the tent.

"He texted me when I got here and said he'll be out in a second. He's in the building behind the tents."

"That's where the guys stay," Sammie chimes in and I smile

to him and his brothers, raising my hand in the air.

"Hi, guys." I wave and they each wave, and then sip their drinks.

"I have to get a drink." Lennon heads to the bar and I'm about to take a seat so I can catch up with Whitney when two arms wrap around my waist.

"How's my girl?" he asks, his lips finding the curve of my neck. As always, goosebumps follow his lips' path.

"She's tired." I swivel around, my arms locking behind his neck. "Someone's been keeping her up late at night."

"Fucker. Tell me who it is and I'll beat his ass." He kisses my lips a little longer than necessary or appropriate given our audience, but isn't that the best part of having a boyfriend? You can kiss him whenever you want and you just don't care what other people have to say about it.

"It's okay, I don't mind."

He presses on my hips and brings me flush against him. For the first time I don't feel his bulging length at my core. I draw back, glancing down at his track pants and t-shirt.

"Cup. I have a cup on, baby," he says with amusement in his eyes. "Which is growing very uncomfortable the longer I stand here." He adjusts himself and I laugh, unhooking my arms.

"Sorry."

"Never be sorry for turning me on." He glances to the bar. "Drink?"

"Sure. But only a beer tonight."

"Did I hear you say beer?" Whitney asks, interrupting our conversation.

"I'm rubbing off on her. Last night she shared a Stella Artois with me and now she's a beer drinker," Lucas jokes and Whitney laughs.

"Let's give her a Miller and see if that still stands," Whitney adds and the joke annoys me. I try not to take it to heart, but I'm not some stuck-up bitch who only drinks champagne.

"You guys want anything?" Lucas asks the table.

"We'll follow you up there," Cole says and signals for Whitney to start walking.

The four us get in a line a few people away from Lennon, who is talking Shawn's ear off. Probably trying to work herself a cut of his profits by promising she'll get more people to place bets with him. If he's smart he'll take her up on that offer.

"Are you nervous?" I ask Lucas and he chuckles.

"No." He shakes his head. "If I was, I wouldn't tell you."

I tilt my head and he laughs.

"I'm your girlfriend," I whine. Aren't we supposed to share everything?

His head dips down and he kisses my nose. "Yes, you are."

"You can tell me anything."

He kisses my temple. "Not anything that makes me sound like a pussy."

"You're crazy." I lay my head on his chest and he wraps his arm around my waist. I bask in his attention. Lately an eight-hour work day seems too long to go without him.

"Spend the night at my place tonight?" he asks and I peer up at him.

"I'd love to."

Lucas hasn't asked me back to his place since I ran out of the diner. I love that he doesn't want to go a night without me.

"Maybe we can have that cinnamon roll in the morning?" he asks.

"I'll buy you one to start your binge week."

He smiles and the flutter in my chest ignites like it always does.

"Sounds like a great Sunday morning." His hand tightens on my hip and I suddenly wish this fight was over and we were back at his place.

"Look, Cole, they're like we used to be," Whitney jokes from behind us and I peek over Lucas's shoulder to look at her.

"It was only weeks ago your tongue was down his throat as you dry-humped him in that chair over there." I point to said chair and she giggles, eyeing Cole in remembrance.

"Touché."

"Whit's obsessing about how the other night we only fucked once and then fell asleep." Cole fills me in with more detail than I need on their sex life. He leans in closer to Lucas and me, lowering his voice an octave. "Warning, that's normal sex, so the dark circles under your eyes and sore pussy aren't permanent."

"I'm not sure about that. Every time I roll over at night I can't help but suck on her tits. Don't see that stopping any time soon." Lucas' crude comment spurs Cole's laughter and causes Whitney to shove her finger in her mouth like she wants to throw up.

"One day you'll be spooning and wonder why your dick isn't hard," Cole adds, thinking everyone's still joking around until he looks over to Whitney. It's clear he's playing with her but you'd never guess it from her pursed lips.

She shoves him in the shoulder and he holds his hands up in the air. "Kidding. I'm kidding, babe." Then his mouth moves to her ear and I watch her face transform from bubblegum-pink to strawberry-pink to puckered and red from whatever he's whispering to her.

Lucas places his arm around my shoulder and kisses the top of my head. "Not us."

I look up at him. "Definitely not us."

⌇

IT'S THE THIRD ROUND and my eyes search out a trashcan because the blood dripping down Lucas' face on to the mat is making my stomach roll. Brock Hayes is back in the ring as his opponent, but it's a very different fight than last time. Especially since Brock's fist just slammed into my boyfriend's temple.

"Kick his ass, Cummings!" Lennon screams next to me.

As for me, I'm like a mute, in awe about how different this scene feels when you care about the person in the ring. He's not the hot guy in red shorts anymore. He's not Raging Bull to me, he's Lucas Cummings, my boyfriend.

Brock hits Lucas and he stumbles back, using the ropes to hold his weight up. His face is pale and his eyes void as though he's two seconds away from passing out.

"Shouldn't they call the fight?" I say, more to myself than anything since the cheering and hollering drowns out my voice.

Lennon moves up to the fence around the ring and screams, "You pussy, get up!"

I think I'll loan her my cheerleading uniform from high school next time. Whitney wraps her arm around my shoulders, pulling me closer to her, probably noticing that I'm chewing on my nails and ruining my manicure. Never a good sign.

"I can barely watch," I say and Whitney rubs up and down on my arm.

"He'll be fine. He's been doing this forever." She tries to give me a pep talk, but it's easy for her to say when it's not Cole getting pummeled up there.

Cole leans forward to add in his opinion. "Don't worry, Tahl. He's beaten him before." Again, why don't we throw him in the ring and see where they weigh in on this topic?

Lucas stands up from the ropes, but he's wobbling back toward Brock. If this wasn't a boxing match, people would assume he'd drunk a bottle of Everclear.

"Isn't there a towel to be thrown in?" I yell over the crowd's cheering.

"Hate to break it to you, but no way would Lucas throw

in the white towel," Cole says.

I point to Cole. "Yes, the white towel. Where is it? I'll throw it in. Actually, I'll choke Brock Hayes with it." I step forward with eyes lasered in on Brock, but Whitney grabs the back of my shirt, rearing me back.

"Now what would the other boys think if Lucas needed his girlfriend to protect him?" Whitney's arm wraps around my shoulders again, her fingers gripping my shoulder too tight for comfort.

"I can't handle this." I hide my face into her neck and she pulls me in tighter. If only she'd cover my ears because all I hear are groans and grunts until there's no question that a body fell to the mat.

"Oh, my God," Whitney says and, having to see for myself, I pry my head from her silk blouse, peeking through the webbing of my fingers.

There lies Lucas on the mat and the referee is counting. Lucas manages to rise up on his knees, but all his movement stalls. I rush to the edge of the fence, squeezing through bodies until I'm next to Lennon.

"Get up, Cummings. You have him. Don't let him embarrass you like this," Lennon screams and I grip her arm, alerting her I'm here. She glances at me and then back to Lucas. "Look, your girl is here and you don't want her to see her wimp of a boyfriend lie down and die, do you? Man up, pussy."

Lucas glances over to me, his face swollen red and dripping with blood. His eyes are laced with despair and hopelessness.

"Lucas," I sigh because seeing a guy who has always been so strong and confident appear beaten down only nauseates my stomach to the point that I might need that trashcan sooner than I thought.

Our eyes lock. The ref's voice, counting down, fades to background noise as Lucas crawls to his feet, flinching and grimacing with each move. My heart leaps and soars out of my chest, through the ropes, right into Lucas' capable hands. In my imagination, of course. I haven't completely lost my mind. Yet.

A cocky smirk crosses his lips, as though he felt the same pull toward me that I did in that brief moment. He's back on his feet, still slightly wobbling. The ref places his finger in front of his face and Lucas' eyes leave mine to follow the ref's finger in the right direction. The crowd roars back to life when the ref steps out of the way and Lucas and Brock are face to face with one another again.

"Go, Cummings!" Lennon shouts, her fist bumping in the air. "Hit him in the balls."

"You got this, Lucas. Kick his ass," I scream next to her and Lennon peers over, unsure if it's me, and then swings her arm around my shoulders with a proud mother look splashed across her face. We both jump up and down yelling, cheering Lucas on.

Five minutes later, Brock is rolling on the mat, unable to get to his feet, and the ref has Lucas' hand in the air, announcing him as the winner. Lennon and I are in hysterics, not holding our excitement down, even with Brock's slutty fan girls glaring at us.

Lucas walks to the edge of the ropes, his beautiful face dripping with blood, but a smile on his face as though he's holding the winning lottery ticket.

"Meet me on the south side of the tent in fifteen minutes," he says and then allows his manager to whisk him away from the mat.

The crowd swallows him up immediately and I quickly lose track of his now sweaty and disheveled blond hair. Lennon and I sit back down at the table with Whitney and Cole. The brothers have a pitcher of beer and Sammie has taken the responsibility to pour everyone a cup.

"He pulled it off, huh?" Sammie says, handing a cup to Cole.

Cole passes it down to us girls. "That was a close one."

"Yeah, too close if you ask us," Todd chimes in and there's some snark in his voice that ignites a protective side of me. I want to crawl over the table and choke him by his tie.

Cole looks past Whitney to me. "Lucas is the house fighter, so they obviously want him to win." He attempts to explain how it all works to me. Although it's new to me, it's information I probably should have asked Lucas about.

Cole continues to drone on and on about the odds, Brock and a bunch of other statistics. The one thing that I do figure out is, if boxing is Lucas' dream and I'm with him, I'll have to understand the standings, the odds and the rankings eventually. But I want to hear it from Lucas' mouth. See the passion in his eyes when he explains to me how high his dreams go.

Glancing at my watch, I realize it's already been fifteen minutes, so I stand and leave the table in search of him. I slide through the groups of people continuing to drink and have fun. Since I was plastered the last time I came here, I don't know how long people stick around after the final fight. Secretly, I hope they all leave soon so I can have the winner to myself.

The closer I get to Lucas, the more my heart flutters. The more butterflies lift in my stomach and the more my skin pinks. How has he won me over so fast? There's no denying it though, I feel something with him that I've never felt before. There's a chance I'd be more crushed if he broke up with me than I was when I called off the wedding with Chase.

I round the corner to the south side of the tent, only to be blinded by a set of headlights. I squint from the brightness and shield my eyes. A woman stands in front of Lucas in the doorway of the building.

He's already in jeans and a t-shirt and his duffle bag rests at his feet. All I can make out of her is her long, curly hair, rain jacket and high heels. She steps closer to him and her arms wrap around his shoulders before she buries her head into the crook of his neck.

That's my spot.

I suck in a breath when I realize that his own arms are just as tight around her waist. I stop in my tracks as I watch their exchange. My entire body feels like it's sinking, as though the concrete parking lot is quicksand.

Somehow I manage a few steps closer. The breeze catches the trees on the street and a flicker of light from the streetlights illuminates their faces. She kisses his cheek and a small smile tugs on his lips. She makes her way back to the passenger side of the car, glances back longingly to him one more time, and then gets in and shuts the door. Before I have a chance to hide, the car passes by me.

Lucas' eyes follow the car's path, catching me standing there gawking. His lips dip down, the smile he had for her disappearing. Picking up his duffle bag, he walks toward me, his shoulders sagging in a way I haven't seen before, and the butterflies in my stomach wilt and die in the pit of my stomach.

TWENTY-FOUR

"**H**EY," HE SAYS, WRAPPING his arm around my waist and kissing my lips. Is he really trying to pretend I didn't see what just happened?

"Hi."

He draws back from the embrace, and the permanent smile that's usually splashed across his lips has vanished.

I run my hand over his bruised and cut face. Will I ever be okay with seeing him like this? Maybe I can't see the person I love get the shit beat out of them every Saturday night. Then again, maybe I don't have to worry about it.

His hand eases mine away and he clasps it in his at our sides. "That was no one."

He's being forthcoming as usual.

"I'm pretty sure it's someone. From the look of the Mercedes, she doesn't do too shabby." I wish I could swallow back the jealousy trying to crawl up my throat. I want to be back in that place where I still believe Lucas can do no wrong.

He steps back, and my hand falls to my side. He shoves his fingers through his wet hair and I wait for his explanation.

"I'm not Chase, Tahlia."

Excuse me?

"What?"

He squares his eyes at me and presses his lips together. "I'm not Chase. That's not some girl I've been fucking." His voice rises an octave.

"I never asked, but I'm fairly sure you'd be asking me who some guy was if I hugged him to my body and kissed his cheek." I cross my arms over my chest. Screw him if he thinks he's about to make this all about my failed engagement.

"I don't need to know every aspect of your life. Did I question you when you were having lunch that day?"

I shake my head as though I care to make sense of where his line of thinking is going. "Yes, you did, and I told you it was business."

"I asked you if it was business or pleasure, that's all."

"Fine. Was *she* business or pleasure?" I ask, knowing that won't be enough to calm the fears creeping into my mind, since he's not giving me a straight answer.

"Business. The only pleasure in my life is you."

Damn him and his words.

Keep it together. Don't let him sweet-talk you.

"I don't kiss my business associates on the cheek nor do I hug them."

He shakes his head and cocks his jaw to the side. "It's complicated, but she was here on business."

My hands go to my hips and I look up to the star-speckled sky, searching for a sign of what to do.

"Promise me," I request, my eyes tearing because there's no way I can handle back-to-back betrayals. I might as well adopt those twenty cats because I'll never trust another guy again. Ever.

He steps forward, his hand dusting my cheek, his thumb prepared to swipe any tears away. My body betrays me and leans into the strength of his hand, the honesty in his eyes.

"Tahlia, I promise, you are the only girl for me. You're the one I wake up thinking about, the one I want to fall asleep with. You're it for me, and it really is that simple." His lips tease a smile and his eyes bore into mine as though wanting to make sure that I see the truth.

"I can't be kept in the dark," I whisper.

"I know. How about I bring you up to speed on all my business?" He smiles and I'm not sure if he's serious or not, but I do need to find out more about this boxing thing and why a girl in a Mercedes would be part of his business.

I nod my head and the smile on his lips gets bigger. "Now, are you going to give me my congratulatory kiss?"

The snap of my fingers would be slower than the speed with which his mood transforms. As much as I'd love to put the issue behind us, I'm scared that I'm on the path to heartbreak once again.

She's still a mystery. A mystery I intend to solve.

A WEEK LATER, I'M waiting in line to risk my life with a harness riding up my ass next to, you guessed it, Aaron.

"Then he told me I could be partner by the time I'm thirty. Can you imagine, partner?"

Aaron's self-inflated ego hasn't changed in the two weeks since I last saw him at a Single in SF event. I nod, my eyes fixed on Lucas, who's at the front of the line, making sure everyone has signed the release papers. Something that should've been done before we were all geared up, but he was late. It's easy to see that he's uneasy with the way he keeps wiping the sweat off his forehead. The bruises and cuts on his face are almost healed, but a few of the people here are commenting as they reach him. Though I've noticed he's distracted because he barely acknowledges the people as they walk through and the guides hook them up on the first zip line.

The night after his win was normal. He took me to his house, we had mind-blowing sex, but those cinnamon rolls didn't happen again because there was a note on the side of the bed saying he'd be right back. I figured he'd gone to grab some and was bringing them back to his apartment, but an hour later he texted me to say he was going to be longer than expected.

Which left me with the question, when is it too early in a relationship to expect to know the whereabouts of your partner all of the time?

That question has been plaguing me the entire week because yep, Lucas has been quiet. Sure, I get a text every morning and every night, but that's where our communication starts and finishes. I had a big client in town so I was unavailable on Tuesday and Wednesday, and then he said he had coaching and training keeping him busy on the other days. If it wasn't for the other night, I could chalk it all up to a scheduling conflict, but that scene unfolds in my mind every night I lie down in my bed alone.

"I told him if he wanted me as partner he'd have to give me an exceptional package." Aaron continues talking as we step one by one to the front.

"Hi, Aaron." Cindy waves, stopping briefly.

"Hello, Cindy." He grants her a small wave. "Then he said I should feel grateful."

I give Cindy a soft smile, but she walks away when Aaron says nothing else to her.

"Aaron," I say.

"I told him there are plenty of firms that would love to have me, so if he wants to make sure I stay committed he better be prepared."

"Aaron."

"He cowered just like I expected. He thought—"

"AARON!" Lucas screams and every one turns their attention to him.

"What?" Aaron asks, not noticing that he's at the front of the line and the guide is hooking him up and giving him instructions.

"It's your turn." Lucas' voice lowers and he glances at me from the corner of his eyes. It's not his usual stolen glance though, but a hesitant one. Almost as if he's unnerved that I'm here in front of him.

"You don't have to yell, Lucas," Aaron says, tossing his hand in the air to the guide rambling instructions about hand placement. "No need. I've done this many times."

Aaron shoots down the zip line and Lucas looks over at the guide. "He's a gold member. Still searching for his perfect match."

The nineteen-year-old guide laughs while he hooks me up.

"Tahlia." Lucas says my name as though he doesn't know my pussy inside and out.

"Lucas." I mimic his tone, wondering why he's suddenly acting like we're not much more than strangers.

The guide swings his hair out of his face and smiles, assuming I caught all his instructions, but I was too busy studying Lucas to hear any advice.

So when he pushes me off the platform my scream echoes off the hills as I fly down the zip line. The harness makes my panties move up my ass crack and all I can wonder is how terrible that must look to everyone behind me. And where am I supposed to put my hands? Are my feet supposed to start going numb like this from hanging here? I peek down below and realize that was a bad idea, so I whip my head back up and stare straight ahead to the next stop to try to keep the image of plunging to my death from hijacking my mind.

The next teenager catches me, I cling to him like I'm four and he's my lost teddy bear. He holds me steady, probably enjoying my tits pressed to his chest until my feet hit the wooden plank. He unclicks my loop and I move to the next one right behind Aaron.

"Did I tell you about the promotion?" Aaron asks and I inwardly roll my eyes, wishing I could twitch my nose and fast-forward this date to the end.

"Yes, you did, but I'm not sure you told Cindy." I swivel him around by his shoulders and have him face Cindy, who just got off the zip line behind me.

Aaron looks back to me and then to Cindy, confused, but once he finally notices her fluttering eyelashes and welcoming smile, his attention focuses in the direction it should. Finally.

The next guide explains the instructions again and the rules are simple. No upside down, as if. Keep hand on brake, who wouldn't? No touching equipment, duh—what if something came off in flight?

Once we're done, the rest of the members move over to the picnic tables where lunch has been spread out for us. Cindy's laughing at Aaron's jokes as the two mosey over that way and I genuinely hope he'll be able to hang up that gold status of his. He might be an annoying gnat, but he's a gnat who would treat a female pretty great, I bet.

I wait, smiling at each of my fellow members who finish the course. Each one passes by me, with their windblown hair and wide smile. The longer it takes, the more I wonder if I shouldn't be standing here, but just when I'm about to go to the picnic tables so I don't appear like some lovesick woman who can't wait twenty minutes to see her guy, Lucas arrives on the plank.

Not needing any instruction, he unhooks his own harness and belt, pulling the clipboard from the back of his shorts. I wish I didn't see the exasperated look on his face when he first spots me because tears start to prick my eyes. Maybe I'm to him what Aaron is to me. Am I Lucas' annoying gnat?

"Tahlia," he says, walking toward me. No excitement. His hands aren't reaching out to touch me, his lips aren't moist and ready to plant on mine. You'd think I'm his colonoscopy doctor from his lack of enthusiasm as he slows his pace. He's about to bypass me and walk by me, but my hand lands on his arm.

"What's going on, Lucas?"

He turns on his heels and blows out a breath of air. "Nothing. You know we can't act like a couple here."

"Oh, I guess I missed that memo after your tongue was shoved down my throat on the yacht. Or when your hands were planted on my ass while we danced that same night. Did you email the rules to me? Maybe it went in my spam folder." I pull out my phone from my back pocket to pretend I'm searching for said email.

"I told you I lost control that night." He glances to the group and then back to me. "Listen." A smile crosses his lips, but not the one usually reserved for me. Not the one that says, *I can't wait to have you naked underneath me.* "I was thinking after this, you come back to my place."

I nod, and inhale a deep breath. "So, my pussy is good enough, just not my conversation skills."

The two teenagers walk by, snickering and laughing when they overhear our conversation.

"Mind your own business," I say and Lucas grabs my hand, leading me away from the group and behind a large tree.

"What is up with you?" he asks.

I shrug out of his hold and wrap my arms around myself from the unexpected chill from his voice. "Nothing."

He cocks those perfect eyebrows. Why are they always so perfect anyway?

"Do you wax or thread?" I ask.

His eyes crinkle and he shakes his head. "What?"

"Your eyebrows, they're perfect. What do you do?"

"You want to talk about my eyebrows?" he asks.

"No, but you aren't going to tell me the truth about what's really going on anyway, so I might as well get one of the answers I'm looking for before you walk away from me." I place my hand on the tree trunk behind me, which forces my breasts to push against the fabric of my shirt.

Lucas' gaze dips and then straightens to my eyes. "I told you I would never lie to you."

"Actually, you told me to trust you."

He blows out a breath and he takes his hat off and then puts it right back on. "And you don't?" My shoulders fall and I stare at him until he speaks. "I know we haven't seen each other this week, but you've been busy."

"Lucas, please don't treat me like an idiot."

He stares over my shoulder instead of directly at me. "Let's just get through this and I'll tell you everything."

"So there *is* something to tell me." My heart rate ramps up to what feels like potential heart attack zone. He steps forward, effectively caging me against the tree with both of his arms. His eyes zoom in on the tight t-shirt that accentuates my breasts and I wonder for a second if he only ever wanted me for sex, but I shrug off that thought. I *know* there are true feelings between us.

"You have nothing to worry about. It's not about another woman. It's a family issue and I hope you see it that way."

He inches closer but I draw back, holding my finger to his lips.

"Pinky-promise me you aren't seeing anyone else."

He laughs, brings up his pinky, squeezing it with mine. "Pinky promise."

"Okay." I let out the breath of air I was holding and my heart falls back into an even rhythm. I know I can handle anything other than another woman. Family issues, who doesn't have them?

"Can I kiss you now?" He bends forward.

"I suppose so."

His lips smash into mine, his tongue urgent and seeking. Just like that our first little tiff is resolved and my hope is renewed. Maybe we really can make this work.

TWENTY-FIVE

"COFFEE?" I ASK LUCAS, procrastinating in the kitchen.

"Come here, Tahl," he says and there's something about him shortening my name that's like being struck by Cupid's arrow.

I round the corner of my breakfast bar and sit beside him on the couch. He takes my hand and entwines our fingers, gripping them tightly.

"The girl in the Mercedes is my sister."

The one thing I've always loved about Lucas is how he always makes sure he stares me in the eyes when he tells something important. Maybe it's second nature for me now to look for the telltale signs of lying. I can only hope he's not a pathological liar who knows exactly what to do to fool me. If only I enjoyed crime movies instead of romantic comedies. The closest thing I've watched to a crime movie is *The Mexican* and I only watched that for Brad Pitt.

"Oh."

"Yeah, Dr. Audrey Campbell." He raises his eyebrows.

"The donor of the parting gifts." I smile, happy to know that the stash of toothbrushes came from his sister, a dentist.

"Actually, they're just for me. She had them made for October in honor of Breast Cancer Awareness Month, but they have the wrong phone number on them, so she gave them all to me."

Well, don't I feel like the idiot in the room. "Sorry."

He cups my chin with his free hand and he brings my gaze up to reach his. "I should have told you that day, but I'm weird about my family. I kept thinking you'd Google her name."

"No. It's okay. I understand being protective."

He shakes his head. "I'm not protective of them. Believe me, they can handle themselves against a hungry pack of wolves. I was protective of you." I squint my eyes, not understanding his full meaning. "Tahl, I broke ties with most of my family five years ago. My mom lives on the East Coast with her new family so she doesn't really miss me. I talk with Audrey, but my dad and I had a huge falling out when I told him I wanted to pursue boxing. I haven't seen him since."

"I'm sorry," I say, feeling saddened for him, but also a little jealous that he had the courage to stick his heels in the ground and do what he loves.

He shrugs. "Believe me, I'm happier without him."

"Why didn't you just tell me? I understand family drama." I inch closer to him, that small river of distrust between us receding.

"There's more. The reason Audrey came to see me Saturday night." He inhales a deep breath and presses his lips together. My stomach knots. I'm assured this is going to be a hammer he's throwing down.

"What?"

"My dad. He's sick. Audrey asked me for a few favors because with the business and her family, she doesn't have the time." He glances at his lap and then turns his attention back to me.

"It's emotionally draining being with him and I knew if I met up with you after seeing him, I'd be an asshole and I couldn't do that to you." He reaches out and caresses my cheek. "I'm sorry for this past week. I'll try to manage between the two."

I swing my legs over his lap, more than ready to push away the polite distance he's keeping. "Is there anything I can do?"

He slinks down on my couch, his hands landing on my hips, and the smile that reaches his eyes is genuine. "No. I'll handle it, but I do want you to know that if I tell you I can't hang out, don't push it, okay? I'd rather be away from you than treat you like shit."

I smile and nod. "Sure." I lean forward and circle my arms around his neck, hugging him tight. "If you want to talk, I'm here, okay?" I whisper in his ear and I feel his head move up and down in my neck.

"Thanks."

We stay like that for a few minutes before I pop up and hold my hand out. He accepts the gesture and stands then takes me in his arms immediately.

"Let's go do something fun," I say.

"Like?" he asks, his lips traveling up my neck.

"Movies, pier?"

"Hmm." He licks up the curve of my neck until he sucks my earlobe into his mouth.

"I'm thinking you have other things in mind?" I ask in a breathy voice. He moans and nods his head, his teeth nibbling on my lobe. "Well, I guess that's fun too." I act nonchalant but inside I'm gearing up for a massive explosion. A whole week away from Lucas makes my lady parts feel lost in a dark, lonely forest.

My earlobe pops out of his mouth and he grips my ass, urging me up. Who am I to argue? My legs wrap around his waist and his lips mesh with mine all the way into my bedroom.

"This will be our own amusement park. I've got one ride in

particular in mind. It's called Bang the Boxer." He winks and my stomach lifts with a million butterflies because Lucas Cummings always keeps his promises.

MONDAYS SUCK.

It's nothing against Monday. If Tuesday was Monday, Tuesday would suck.

I haven't had my coffee this morning. My boyfriend is an amazing guy. He's sweet, endearing, loving. He can give me five orgasms in one night, beat the shit out his opponent in the boxing ring, but coffee-making? Not his forte. Starbucks won't be looking for him anytime in the future, that's for sure.

Plus, he was still sleeping as I snuck out this morning. He's had to be with his dad more than he'd prefer recently since Audrey had to fly out to a dentist convention in Miami. I wonder what dentists talk about at their conventions? Tartar, cavities and root canals don't sound very interesting.

"Grande black," I tell the barista at the same time my phone rings. I ignore it, much to the exasperation of the man behind me. Would he rather me delay him longer by answering it? I pay, move to the pick-up area and finally dig out my phone.

My dad. Hmm.

"Tahlia," the barista calls out.

I grab my coffee and move to the cream and sugar area to make it exactly how I love it—a splash of skim and two sugar packets. Once my mind is ignited after a few sips of coffee, I call my dad back.

"Hey, Dad, what's up?" I ask and he huffs.

"The sun, Tahlia, that's what's up. Can you please talk professionally?"

I roll my eyes, sipping my coffee once again. "Yes, Father,

how can I assist you on this beautiful morning?" I say in my most high-society pleasant voice.

Another huff rings over the line.

"Listen. I just got news. Hugh Tavern passed away this morning." I hear papers shuffling around him and his secretary is whispering on the other end. "Hold on, Tahlia . . . yes, a big arrangement once we hear what the funeral plans are."

"How? That's sad." My footsteps move into overtime to reach the office in record speed because this is a game-changer.

Hugh Tavern owns Tavern Meats and Selections and they are Santora Sausage's biggest competitor in North America.

"I didn't play golf with the man, Tahlia."

I roll my eyes since he can't see me and ask, "Who told you?"

"Turn off your dumb shows about roses and bachelors and turn on CNN. You'd be amazed by what you find out." His office phone rings. "Listen, hurry in. We'll have to go to the funeral for appearances."

AKA we'll have to go to make sure that their clients know Santora Sausage cares and we're still around if they're thinking of jumping ship.

"Okay, I'm on Vine and—"

The line dies and I hold it out to see, sure enough, he hung up on me.

Who's the one who should be preaching about phone etiquette now, Dad?

By the time I make it into my office, Midge has printed out the articles about Hugh Tavern and placed them on my desk . . . per my father's request, I'm positive. Another coffee with milk and sugar packets are placed next to them like always. Midge is a gem and I'll never sacrifice her.

Without meaning to, I wonder if she'd risk her employment and come work for me if I ever had the guts to do the party-planning venture. I shake my head at the absurdity because who am

I kidding? I'll never risk it.

Once I read the articles, I walk down to my dad's office to discuss our plan for Operation Tavern. It's sad really. That a man dies and the company he built is now dissected to figure out how to grab the clients before the first shovel of dirt hits his casket.

Lo and behold, Michael Plotter is sitting front and center in front of my dad.

"Good morning," I say.

"Not for Hugh Tavern," Michael says and I give him a look of disgust because I never liked Hugh either, but the comment is crude.

I sit down, cross my legs and sip the last of my Starbucks coffee.

My dad stops typing on his keyboard and graces us with his full attention. Me, Michael and five other vice-presidents await the plan from their CEO.

"So Tahlia and I will be attending the funeral. It's already been planned for Thursday. We'll go to the burial and back to the Taverns' estate for drinks and the catered meal."

"What about me?" Michael asks. You'd think we're in gym class and he's the last one to be picked from the whine in his voice.

"It will be more heartfelt if it's just the Santora family that attends." My dad looks at me and I nod that he can count on me. "We'll report back with the lists of clients who attend and after a week, we'll make contact with them."

As sick as his plan is, I know this is my dad's fear. That one day someone will be coming to his funeral not to mourn him but to swallow up the business that's put every white hair on his head.

"Who's taking over Tavern?" Michael asks and my dad shrugs his shoulders.

"I'm not sure. Last I heard his brother maybe. That's

something we need to find out though, so go ahead and do the digging, Michael."

Michael smiles like a middle child finally getting praise from their parent. "I'm on it."

I shake my head.

"That's all for now. The rest of you can go, but Tahlia, I'd like you to stay."

I stand to help myself to a coffee, knowing this conversation has been coming for a while. I'm not naive enough to think Tavern's death isn't going to make my dad start dissecting his own company.

The room empties and my father asks his assistant to shut the door behind her. And then it's just me and my dad. Let the uncomfortableness begin.

"We need to talk," my dad says, rounding his desk toward the couch and chair.

I sit on the couch, he sits in the chair, our usual positions. I place my coffee down and cross my legs and wait for his lecture.

"I need to know where you stand with the company."

I shouldn't be surprised by my dad's forwardness, but I am. I'm caught off guard because I don't have an answer. Especially the answer he wants. "I'm here."

He eyes me long and hard. "Tahlia."

"Honestly?" I ask, and suck in a deep breath. It may be my last.

"You don't want to take over this company, do you?" He releases the pressure of me having to toss it out there like a half-dead fish slapping up and down on the table in front of us.

"No, but I will. Dad, Santora Sausage means everything to you and the family and I don't want to disappoint—"

"Stop, Tahlia." His eyes fix on his hands clasped in his lap.

"Okay." I sink into the black leather couch.

"I know your heart isn't in this company, but I brought in Michael as an option. I'm going to ask you for a favor."

"Anything." With the hurt in my father's eyes, my dream of party planning doesn't sound so thrilling. Being selfish and abandoning my father and family isn't worth happiness.

"Leave."

"No. I'm not going to leave the company. I mean, Dad." My head shakes vehemently. "No way."

"Do you think when I was growing up, I thought I'd lead a sausage company?" he asks and I'm thinking he felt the same obligation I did. Noticing my confused face, he continues, "Well, yeah, of course I knew it was what I was going to do, but I wanted to be a doctor."

"A doctor?"

He nods. "Yeah, but as you know Grandpa died before I ever finished undergrad, so here I am." He holds his hands out to his sides.

"Not too shabby though."

"Nope." A small smile graces his lips. I'll always be proud and amazed of what my father has accomplished here with no mentor to guide him. "But it's not an operating room either." I nod, understanding exactly what he's saying. "I never want to do that to you and selfishly, I have been. I thought maybe you'd start to love it and get some fire in your belly for this place, but I see you in the halls. Sure, you smile, you're organized. You've given a hundred percent, but you're not happy. And that's what's most important to me." He stands and moves to pour his own cup of coffee. "Tavern has children, did you know?"

I cock my head, not sure where he's going with this. "He has a kid he never talks to because he didn't want part of the business." My father turns around with his cup of coffee in his hand. "I think your mother would kill me if one day you decide to run away just to escape me and this company."

Relief wars with guilt inside of me. "Dad," I say with as much disbelief as I feel right now. Never would I have ever guessed that my dad would offer me a free pass.

He shakes his head. "No, Tahlia. You deserve to be happy in your life and if party planning is what you want to do, then pursue it. Don't worry about your mother. I'll deal with her. The company is going to let you go with six months' severance pay. Sound good?"

I smile with tears in my eyes and slide to the edge of the seat. "More than good, Dad." I stand but he shoos me back down with his hand, knowing exactly what I'm going to do.

"Don't, Tahlia," he says at the same moment my arms wrap around his neck.

"You're so awesome, Dad. Thank you." I hug him tight to my body and eventually his own arms move around me. "I love you."

"I love you." His body grows stiff. He's never been comfortable with affection. "Now, sit down and tell me your plans. You aren't going to keep many clients if you're answering the phone with, 'What's up?'"

I laugh, the weight of all the pressure I've been carrying around for years lifting off my shoulders. "Plans?" I move to the couch and he cocks his eyebrow at me.

"Tahlia, I bet you already have a business plan written up." He takes a seat across from me and for the first time at sausage headquarters, as Lennon refers to it, I'm excited and inspired about my future.

TWENTY-SIX

I CHOSE TO WEAR a conservative black dress, black nylons, and black heels, and my hair is pulled back in a low, neat ponytail. If I can do anything for my father before I leave Santora Sausage it's to be the epitome of a good executive while attending his biggest competitor's funeral. I park in front of my parents' house since we're to ride in a limo together there and back. To showcase what a close-knit family we are.

My phone rings while I take the keys out of the ignition.

Lucas.

A smile appears on my lips because the past few nights, Lucas' hands won't leave my body. He wants me constantly, anytime and anywhere he can have me. There's been no delicate hands or lovemaking, it's pure animalistic sex and I love it. I crave it. Not to say that I don't enjoy making love to the man, but there's something about the passion that burns in his eyes lately that I can't get enough of.

"I'm in black," I answer.

"Lace?"

"Panties, yes."

"Hmm . . . keep going, A visual is starting."

"What else do you need?" I ask, climbing out of my car.

"Bra?"

"What bra?" I joke and although he doesn't laugh, I hear a strangled breath over the receiver.

"You *will* kill me one day," he says. I laugh a little then pick up on the fact that there's a lot of background noise behind him.

"Where are you?" I ask, taking a few steps toward my parents' front door.

A huge breath leaves his lips. "I'm going to be gone a few days," he says. "Think you can live without me until Monday?"

"I suppose I'll survive. Where are you going?" I ask, disappointment quickly setting in that for the first time in weeks I'll be alone on a weekend.

"I'll be local, but I just won't have time to see you." A kid cries behind him, but he must move somewhere else because the sound is gone quickly.

"Is it your dad?" I turn on the front stoop when I hear a car behind me. A limo pulls up into the circular driveway.

"Yeah." His voice is tinged with exhaustion, sadness and something else I can't place.

"Let me come. I promise I'll be on my best behavior." I hold up my Girl Scout fingers even though he can't see them.

"Thanks, but I got this. Monday night, your place, no clothes?" He changes the subject quickly and I can't help but think he's rushing me off the phone.

"Okay. Call me?"

"I'll try, but know I'm thinking about you." The phone clicks as my parents' front door opens in front of me before I can say anything else and my shoulders slump as I wonder why he's so hell-bent on dealing with this without me.

"Who killed your puppy?" Caterina says, joining me outside.

"Nice of you to look so elegant." My eyes fixate on her

black hat.

"It's vintage," she says, rolling those blue eyes of hers.

"It's ugly," I comment and step over to the limo and slide inside.

"Where are your glasses, librarian?" she sneers back, but I situate myself in the seat, ignoring her.

"Tahlia," my mother coos, joining us a minute later. "You look beautiful." I smile at Caterina in a smug ha.

"Thank you, Mom. You, too." She does, but no one can dress for an occasion better than my mother can.

She's wearing a hat similar to Caterina's, but hers is conservative with a wide brim. No netting or bows like Cat's, which looks similar to the start of a bird's nest.

A few minutes later my dad joins us and we head out to the service. My mom bothers Caterina the entire ride about her need to get a summer job. That she won't find her husband sitting by the pool everyday, how she's starting college in the fall and she needs to get some real-world experience. I add in my two cents a few times just to piss her off more, because that's what sisters do.

The limo arrives at Tavern Estates and the bickering conversation between my mom and Cat continues. I'm not sure the Academy Awards has this many limos. Hugh Tavern is being buried in the family plot that's tucked away on their property. Inch by inch we drive up the long road and a half hour later, the tree line breaks and there stands a mansion double the size of my family's. Grey brick with white pillars. Black double doors up a staircase. It's gorgeous and cold all entwined. Nothing about it feels like a cozy family home where loved ones gather. It comes off as more of a showpiece than anything.

We're shuffled to golf carts before I can have a better look at the house, but the landscape is impeccable with neatly shaped trees. There are no flowers, though. I don't know why I notice, but all that gorgeous landscaping and not one flower in the height of spring.

"Watch out for the birds," I whisper to Caterina and she scoffs. "You don't want one thinking your hat is a bird's nest and landing on it."

"Don't get lost, they might take you back to the church with the other nuns."

"Oh, Cat." I point to a bird flying the sky. "Take cover before it head-dives."

"Behave, the two of you," my mom whispers from the row behind us.

Knowing I better stop because we're supposed to be the perfect Santoras at this function, I don't taunt Caterina any further. We're supposed to have class, dignity and a family bond. So, when the golf cart stops, I swing my arm though Caterina's and we walk side by side as though we're the best of friends. We're sisters, yes, and we love each other, yes, but with such a large age gap between us we've never had the best relationship. When I was a teenager she was a bratty little kid who was always trying to insert herself into my life. I'm hopeful that as she gets older and matures our relationship will improve, but I'm not holding my breath.

A cute guy Caterina can't stop staring at escorts us to our seats. The casket is raised on the pulleys, ready to be lowered into the ground, and there's a giant picture of him with, again, no flowers. What do the Taverns have against flowers? Without the usual cascade of roses across the casket it appears cold and foreboding.

Instead there are picture frames perched on top of the gleaming wood. I note that it's just him in the pictures, at various points of his life. No family. How sad.

The seats fill in and I pull my phone from my purse to silence it when the priest stands at the podium.

"Talk about a hot ass," Caterina says, nudging me with her elbow. "You only wish you could get a guy like that." Her head nods but when I look up no one is there.

"Where?" I whisper.

"He sat down. I think he must be family, but damn, I might have to make my move at the reception." Her eyes stay glued to the area, but I can't see anything over the lady in front of me who must have bought her hat at the same place as Caterina.

An hour later, I shift in my seat. Wooden white chairs are not meant to be sat in for this long. There wasn't even a eulogy. The priest only talked about him and how he grew this company and I swear it comes off like Hugh Tavern wrote it himself.

The priest asks everyone to stand and the front row circles around the back of the casket. A school-aged boy holds hands with a man who must be his father who has another toddler in his arms. A woman who has faint tears falling from her eyes allows the comfort of another man next to her, his arm wrapped around her shoulders. When they've made their way around the casket they turn to face the crowd and all the air in my lungs ceases to exist as I struggle to breathe.

Caterina nudges me. "See? Told you," she whispers.

I blink.

I blink again.

I blink a third time.

I have to be seeing things because it's Lucas comforting that woman.

My Lucas.

"Lucas Tavern, along with his sister and brother-in-law, Audrey and Travis Campbell, would like you all to join them for a reception in the dining room," the priest says after the prayer is finished.

No way.

Lucas Cummings is Lucas Tavern?

My legs feel weak and my throat tightens. I can't seem to get enough oxygen in my lungs so I sit down on my chair while mentally dissecting every bit of information he's told me.

Did I miss something somewhere? The sandwich shop? No. When he talked about his father's disapproval? No. He never mentioned this to me and I know I'd remember. I mean Santora Sausage and Tavern Meats have been competing since forever.

The fact that my shock can morph into anger faster than lightning scares me because that's what I feel now. Red-hot rage twists my insides and I clench my hands in my lap.

"Tahlia, darling." My dad urges me to leave the row since it's our turn.

I stand and slide out of my aisle, glancing over my shoulder, finding Lucas still there, watching his father's body lower to the ground. I stop and turn, causing Caterina to run into my back.

"Walk much?" she sneers.

I don't answer but watch Lucas' chest rise and fall with labored breaths. I take a step in his direction, my feet moving of their own accord. The pain on his face shows in his tight lips, his eyes closing and opening. He's pushing back his tears.

"That must be the son," my father says, swiveling me around and leading me to the golf carts. "I can't imagine how he feels." My dad continues to talk on the way to the golf cart. "Michael found out the company has been left to him."

"What?" My voice is hollow.

"Tavern Meats and Selections is his even though he doesn't want it. It might be time for me to make a bold move." My dad's lips turn up before he grows serious again. "Today isn't the day for us to talk business though."

We reach the golf cart and I take a seat, my gaze once again fixating on Lucas. At the same time the golf cart drives off, he turns around and walks the opposite way, his hands stuffed into his pockets and his shoulders sagging as he descends a hill away from where everyone else is headed.

A half hour into the reception and the room is packed while I pace outside the front entrance, waiting for what, I'm not sure. Lucas hasn't arrived, although I guess he could have gone in through a back door. Who knows how many entrances this mansion has?

The urge to go in there screaming and yelling that he lied to me burns in my belly. He's always been truthful. At least I thought so. I trusted him and now my fragile heart breaks for him and because of him all the same.

I walk toward the door, the handle in my hand, but shake my head and turn around. My dad gave me an out from the company. I can't repay him by spitting in his face, which is exactly what I'd be doing if I made a scene. I'm not sure if it's luck or not, but Lucas opens the front door, not seeming at all surprised to see me standing there. Without a word, he grasps my upper arm and guides me to the garage.

I shrug out of his hold but he grabs my arm again, this time with more strength than he's ever used with me, not letting go until we're behind closed doors. Closed doors that hide about ten vintage, restored cars.

"Go ahead," he says, sitting on a stool in front of a pristine-looking work bench, fiddling with his keys.

"What?" I ask, confused.

"Go ahead. Yell, scream, whatever you want to do." There's no emotion in his voice and somehow that makes all this worse.

"How could you have lied to me?"

"How could I have told you?"

"You told me you'd never lie." The words leave my lips in a hoarse whisper.

"I never lied."

"A lie by omission is still a lie, Lucas," I say.

He concentrates on the keys in his hand. "Come for a drive

with me."

"No. I don't know you." I pace across the concrete floor.

"You know me."

I stop, looking him square in the eye. "I don't know you, Lucas. Your last name isn't even Cummings. You're one of *them*." My mind floods and I can't reason fast enough. "You're a silver-spoon kid. One who's gotten everything he ever wanted. I'm such an idiot. Well, good act, Lucas *Tavern*. You sure fooled me."

He stands and steps over to me. Tears start to brim my eyes when he places his hands on my shoulders. Everything that I believed about him is a lie.

"Tahl, I *am* Lucas Cummings. I left my family five years ago and I changed my name because I didn't want anyone to judge me based on my last name. Surely you understand that."

I brush his hands off me. "You could have told me the truth. You acted like you were just some average Joe, but you're a billionaire."

"My dad is a billionaire."

"And now you are. I heard the company is yours. Congratulations." I hit myself in the forehead. How stupid could I have been? "You got close to me because I'm a Santora! It's all an act, isn't it? You only befriended me because you knew who I was and you thought you could get some kind of inside dirt on the company."

"No," he bites out. He closes the gap between us and I'm blocked from behind by an SUV of some type. His hands clasp on my cheeks, our eyes meeting. "I fell in love with you and I was scared shitless that you wouldn't accept this part of my past."

"You lied, Lucas."

I swallow down the exhilaration of hearing 'I love you' from his lips. This morning there was nothing I wanted to hear more, but I don't want to be told like this. Not when he's taken a sledgehammer to my heart and left it in pieces. There's nothing left to beat for him and so his declaration only makes me feel . . . empty.

"I know. I tried so many times. I've been as honest as I can be. I didn't want this company. I didn't want this life. I figured once he was buried, you'd never have to worry about it after I sign the company over."

I shake my head. "I have no idea if you're telling the truth."

"I am."

"You're Lucas Tavern," I say more for myself than to him, still astonished at this information. I stare at the floor, my mind reeling, too many thoughts whizzing by to try to make sense of any of them. "I have to go." I rush to the door, but he's there with his hand on the handle before I can open it.

"I love you, Tahlia. I'd love you whether your last name was Santora or otherwise. I'm the guy you think I am. The one who lives in an apartment above a boxing gym and works for every penny he spends. The fact that I was born with a different last name shouldn't matter. Please, we can work this out," he whispers, his voice breaking.

"See, that's the problem with lies, Lucas. You tell one and they taint everything that comes out of your mouth . . . even if it is the truth. I don't know that I can ever trust you again."

He sighs, his hand falling from the door.

I open it but he slams it shut again. He swings me around so our eyes lock. Then he smashes his lips to mine, his tongue parting my lips and sliding in to touch mine. For a brief few seconds, I'm lost in the love of Lucas Cummings, matching his fevered pace. Physical sparks were never our problem. My hands move up to his hard chest and I push him off me.

"I'm sorry," I say and open the door, needing to put some distance between myself and the man I'm not sure I can live with, but whom I feel I can't live without.

TWENTY-SEVEN

A WEEK THAT FEELS like a year later, I walk into my office to find Michael sitting in my desk chair. "Midge, please call security," I say as I enter, taking off my coat and then placing it on the coat hook.

He smiles. "Just seeing how my new office will feel." He leans back in his chair. "Would you like me to box up your items for you?" he asks.

I roll my eyes, sitting down in the chair across from him. I loathe him, but maybe he's the right fit for this company, though I worry about his loyalty and trustworthiness. A knock sounds on the door and I turn to find Midge.

"Miss Santora, your father just called a meeting in the conference room. He'd like both you and Mr. Plotter to attend." She waits for our answer, like either one of us would decline.

"Thanks, Midge."

Michael stands and then holds out his arm. "After you, princess," he says.

I stand, grabbing my phone, a pad and a pen.

"Party planning, huh?" Michael asks on the way to the

conference room.

"Yep."

"You'll have no nights or weekends for yourself."

I shrug and keep walking. "Maybe."

"Your Saturday nights will always be booked."

A sharp pang invades my chest. "I should press pause on my dating life anyway."

"Damn, and I was going to try my luck again."

We hit the conference room doors and I swing around to look at him. "Sorry, you're not my type." I open the door while still looking behind me at Michael and he comes to an abrupt stop, his eyes wide. I turn and glance around the conference room wondering what's caught him by surprise.

Lucas is here.

My stomach plummets and my mouth dries up so much that only the tall drink of water sitting across from my father would be able to quench it. Before Lucas can see my reaction to his presence I straighten my back and walk all the way in.

"What is *he* doing here?" I sneer, uncaring if my father picks up on my animosity toward his visitor.

"Tahlia, sit," my dad says, patting the spot next to him which will leave me right across from Lucas.

"Let me get some coffee first." I walk toward the coffee station, needing to buy a few seconds to compose myself. I haven't seen him since his father's funeral and though I've found myself wanting to reach out to him, missing him desperately, I haven't. He made his choices and I'm not sure I can accept them.

"Hurry, please. I have business to attend to," my dad comments.

"Isn't this meeting about business?" I ask.

"Don't be smart, Tahlia. Michael, sit down next to Lucas."

Michael skittishly slides into his seat like he's late for geometry. That cocky flair he usually walks with is long gone.

Lucas raises from his chair and a second later he's beside me. "Allow me." Lucas picks up the coffee pot and pours me a cup.

"Thank you," I manage to squeeze out, trying to ignore the smell of his usual scent, soap and musk, and all the happy memories I attach to that smell.

My hand moves for the milk, but he quickly grabs it.

"I'll do it." He tilts it toward my cup.

He might have destroyed my faith in men, he might have destroyed my heart, but he will not destroy my coffee. "I don't think so." I hold my hand out for him to pass it, which he doesn't.

Instead he splashes some in my cup. I huff and a low chuckle leaves his throat.

Jackass.

Before I have the chance to grab two sugar packets, he has two in his hand.

Stubborn jackass.

Ignoring his offer, I reach in front of him, blocking his access to my cup.

"Oh, you take sugar, too?" I ask and he laughs again and rips the two packets at the same time I rip mine.

We both end up dumping the packets into my cup, effectively ruining my coffee.

"Uh," I mumble.

"I'll take that one," he says, moving his hand over to take it.

"Forget it. I don't need coffee that badly anyway." I stalk off and sit down next to my father.

"Whenever you're ready, Lucas," my dad says in a way sweeter voice than he'd use with me.

"Yeah, no rush." I roll my eyes and my dad glances over to me with furrowed brows. "Take your time. I'm sure you have nowhere to be."

While Lucas makes us wait, I tap my foot and realize Michael is sweating. He grabs a napkin and blots his forehead and he looks like he's swallowing a hair ball or something with the way his Adam's apple keeps moving.

"You okay?" I ask and he nods his head unconvincingly.

"Here," Lucas says, sliding a coffee cup in front of me.

I glance at the color and it looks similar to my usual concoction. "Thank you," I say, sitting up straighter in my chair and taking a sip.

Damn him. It's perfect.

He raises his eyebrows at me, implying that I should trust him to make me a cup of coffee.

Whatever.

Lucas slides into the chair across from me, unbuttoning his suit jacket before he sits. It's a practiced move, one he looks like he's done a million times before, and it tells me that he's used to clothes like that. No surprise there, I suppose. He probably grew up wearing suits every day.

"So, we have two agendas today, and only one needs your attention. Michael." My dad glares over at an already antsy Michael.

"Yes, sir." Michael's back straightens to attention with my dad's voice.

My eyes ping-pong between the two of them as I wonder what the hell is going on, but I can't help noticing the smug look on Lucas's face.

"You should be extremely happy that Mr. Tavern came to me directly. Otherwise, you'd be whisked away in handcuffs right now. I've been informed that you approached Lucas and told him things about Santora Sausage that were confidential in the hopes of gaining employment at his company. I suppose until you found out that Tahlia is leaving the company you thought your opportunities were better elsewhere. Not to worry, you're free to do what you like now. Effective immediately, your employment here is terminated."

A knock sounds on the door and my father's assistant opens the door for two security personnel.

"He's lying! I was trying to get an in with their company." Michael's gaze swings to Lucas. "He's a no one, a guy who had his whole life handed to him and he walked away from it. You can't trust what he says." The security personnel pry him up from the chair and my eyes widen as I glance from my dad to Michael, purposely diverting my gaze away from Lucas.

"One last piece of advice, Michael. If you ever want to run a company, don't underestimate those around you. Did you really think I didn't know that Hugh Tavern had a son that the company was going to be handed down to? Good luck in your future endeavors and don't use me as a reference." Michael begins to reply but my dad holds his hand up in the air. "That is all." He nods to the security guards and they drag Michael with them as they exit.

"Whoa," I say. "What a week full of surprises. Must be my birthday or something." This time I allow my eyes to land on Lucas, who cocks his jaw to the side.

"Rhonda, will you please excuse us," my dad says to his assistant, who is still standing at the door.

She nods and files out of the room, shutting the door behind her. My dad stands to make his own cup of coffee.

I sip mine. Damn him. Lucas might not be able to make good coffee, but he knows how to mix my perfect cup.

That cocky grin appears again, so I place the cup down and slide it across the table.

"Oh, come on. You won't even drink the coffee I made you?" Lucas whispers over the table.

"Tainted," I say.

"I want to talk," he says, leaning forward. "Clear the air between us."

"No," I mouth because now that I've calmed down a bit I

don't want my dad to know we were together.

He tilts his head and gives me puppy dog eyes, silently begging me to get over the anger and to move into makeup phase.

"So, Tahlia. I understand you already know Lucas." My dad sits down with his coffee.

I guess not trying to let my dad know Lucas and I were a thing was a wasted effort. I glare at Lucas and cross my arms over my chest. "Not this version."

Lucas huffs and the tiniest bit of guilt invades me for a second. Then I push it aside because I'm not the one who hid who I am.

"I'm going to apologize for my daughter. She gets this stubborn side from her mother." My dad laughs and I turn to look at him, narrowing my eyes.

"Dad, you do understand that he lied to me?"

"I do." He nods and looks at Lucas. "But I think you need to hear him out."

"Whatever."

"Tahlia, you're not a teenager, nor should you talk like one."

I swear I'm a second away from stomping out of here in true sixteen-year-old girl fashion. "Why are you involved in our business?" I ask my dad, pointing between Lucas and me.

"Tavern and Santora are going to merge," my dad announces and Lucas' gaze falls to the table.

"See." I stand up. "You were into me just for my family's company. I knew it." I start circling the table like a hawk hunting its next meal. "You only wanted me because of my last name."

Lucas stands, his chair slamming against the wall, and he stalks toward me. Grabbing both my upper arms, he stops me from moving.

"Damn it, Tahlia. Listen for once before jumping to conclusions. Did I know who you were? I did. Let's remember I pieced that information together after *you* lied to me and said you were a Pilates instructor." I glance over to my father for a beat, feeling ashamed for initially lying about my job. "I tried to stay away from you."

"Well, you did a piss-poor job of it." I roll my eyes, jutting out a hip.

"You're right, I did. After that night on the boat, I hit up Google after Chase referred to you as the sausage queen. And I was going to stay away. I was. But I couldn't stop thinking about you. I needed to see you one last time and then when I saw you leave Santora's building with that dipshit, I couldn't keep my distance."

"Convenient, don't you think?"

His hands leave my skin and he throws them up in the air. "You're impossible."

"Tahlia, sit down." My dad uses his stern parenting voice and I feel like I'm thirteen again, and just had a hair tugging fight with Caterina.

I sit down and Lucas changes seats to sit in the one right next to me. He positions his chair to face me and takes my hands in his, staring into my eyes.

"I fell in love with *you*, Tahlia. But you made it known that what you loved about me was that I didn't have money, I didn't have clout. I took you to that speakeasy and you weren't impressed. You wanted to leave and do something that cost me barely anything. So I did, but in that moment I knew that if I told you, I risked losing you. When Audrey met me after the fight to tell me how ill my father had become, I didn't know what to do."

"You could have told me, Lucas," I say, surprised at how calm my voice is.

"My entire life was crumbling. I knew he was going to leave the company to me. It was always important to him that it stay in the family. It was his last failed attempt to keep me involved. I was trying to figure it all out, but in truth, I should have told you. I can see that now. If I lose you because of that, then I will live my life with that as my biggest regret. But I don't want to lose you." He pauses for a second. "I need to know . . . do you love me?" he asks.

I look up into those green eyes, filled with a hope I'm not sure lives within me anymore. No matter how badly I want to lie, I'd only be a hypocrite. "I do," I admit for the first time out loud. Even myself.

"Then that's all we need."

"Lucas," I sigh. Tears prick the corners of my eyes and I suck in a sharp breath to try to keep them from falling.

He hangs his head for a second and then shifts his gaze to my father and back to me. He stands, his eyes losing the hope that filled them moments ago. Just like that he buttons up his jacket and walks away from me.

"I'll call you tomorrow, Bill."

He walks out of the conference room and I know without a doubt that my biggest regret is that I couldn't give him the answer he wanted.

TWENTY-EIGHT

I'M PATHETIC. IT'S BEEN a week and a half and I've picked up my phone a half dozen times to call Lucas. Okay, maybe a hundred, but you get the gist. I cried for a day, ate ice cream for two, sulked for three, drowned in romantic comedies for four, but now I want him again. He's like a drug, damn it, and he's made me addicted to him. Probably used some voodoo shit on me in my sleep.

My latest masochistic endeavor is Googling everything about him. Turns out when his parents divorced, he moved with his mom to Boston for high school. Attended Harvard and then came back to San Francisco for some reason and started boxing a few months after graduation. That's all I've pieced together so far.

A knock sounds on my door and I think to myself that I really should just give the girls a key because they're here often enough. I stand and trudge slowly to open the door.

Lennon barrels in with brown paper bags I'm assuming means I'm being gifted another vibrator. With Lucas' help, I haven't really needed one lately. I guess that ship has sailed.

"At least you aren't wearing those hideous clothes you were

wearing after Chase." Her nose scrunches.

"More sex toys?" I ask dryly and follow her down the hall.

She flutters her eyelashes. "Yes, but I have something so much better." She throws a DVD on my breakfast bar.

I pick it up. "*Grease Two*," I say.

She busies herself in my kitchen, grabbing drinks and popping popcorn in my microwave. When she's done we go sit in my living room.

"Where's Whit?" I ask, crossing my legs on the couch, figuring I'll deal with Lennon's crap for a while. It's better than being stuck in my own head.

"She sends her love, but she's working a story and doesn't have time to deal with your pathetic ass."

"Pathetic ass?" I question and she places the bowl of popcorn between us and then sits on the other side.

"You didn't put the movie in. Fine," she huffs. "I'll do it." She rises from her seat, puts in the DVD in my player and grabs the remote.

"Can we go back to you calling me a pathetic ass?"

"We could, you'll get the meaning after we watch the movie. Now, be quiet and use those magna cum laude ears because this is the only way I can snap you out of this."

"What—"

"Psst." She places her hand in front of my face.

"Fine. Whatever."

I think I really need to expand on my vocabulary soon because I am starting to sound like I should be hanging out at the mall, popping my bubblegum with Cat and her friends.

The movie begins and my shoulders start moving back and forth. Lennon glares at me. I'm not sure why she picked this movie because musicals are definitely not her thing.

I become engrossed in the movie as I push the memories of Lucas and I watching *Grease* together as far back in my mind as possible. I start to loathe Lennon for pulling this memory back to the surface until I realize he will not ruin my love of romantic movies.

The credits roll and Lennon clicks the television off and I decide not to tell her that she ate the whole bowl of popcorn on her own.

"So?" she asks and I raise my eyebrows.

"So." I clasp my hands together in my lap.

"Have you seen the light?"

"The light?" I ask, completely unfazed by the movie or whatever meaning she was trying to get me to extract. "Oh, you mean, if I don't date a T-bird I might not be able to be a pink lady? Or that I shouldn't judge others by their outward appearance?"

"See, you do get it." She points to me.

"What?"

"You judged Lucas on his outward appearance."

"Um, no. I wouldn't have gone home with him if that was the case, Len." I pick the pieces of broken popcorn up off the couch and place them in the empty bowl.

"So you didn't get the point?" Lennon asks, stopping me from picking up her mess. She waits until I look up at her. "I get that Chase hurt you, and I tried not to punch him in the nuts for the sake of Cole, because I'm sure he wants to be an uncle someday, but don't let him ruin what you have with Lucas."

When I see her so serious, tears well up in my eyes. "He's no better than Chase."

She tilts her head to the side. "We both know that's not true. Did he lie? He did, but just like Michael Carrington tried to hide who he was to get Stephanie's attention. He did it because he wanted to be the man you want."

I shake my head. "You're wrong. He omitted information. Very pertinent information."

"That he came from billions?"

"That he comes from my family's biggest competitor."

"Tahl." She says my name so soft, one tear escapes my eye. "I know you love him. He did lie, but punish him by making him eat you out until you take your final breath. Or don't give him any blow jobs for a year. You could even take away sex altogether, but I have to say that I think you're really just punishing yourself there. My point is, *don't* punish him by putting an end to what you two had. He needs a second chance and I think we both know that."

I shrug.

"He's made good, even on the family business front."

"How do you know that?"

"The MSNBC. How else am I going to make sure my sex toy company is going to make a profit?"

"They're talking about the merger on MSNBC?" I ask and she nods.

"Can I say I thought he filled out a pair of boxing shorts? Man, in a suit, the man is downright edible. You know how many ladies will be ready to claim him?"

"They can have the liar." I stand, unable to sit anymore.

Lennon grabs my forearm and drags me back down to the couch. "Stop, Tahlia. Just stop." Her voice is even more authoritative and it's kind of *Mommie Dearest* scary. "Just stop focusing on the lying. Start looking at what you're throwing away and ask yourself, are the reasons you want to really worth it?" She blows out a stream of air and looks up to the ceiling. "I know you aren't this dense."

I sit there rethinking everything that happened with Lucas. "I do miss him," I say, hating myself for the admission.

"See. What do you miss?"

"I miss having him next to me in bed."

"What else?" she asks, inching closer.

"I miss the way he always held my hand or wrapped his arm

around me. Like he was announcing to the world that I was his."

"He did have the alpha thing down pat. Anything else?"

My mind wanders back to our time together. "The way I felt safe with him. Like nothing bad could happen to me."

"It's safe to say he'd wrestle a hippopotamus for you."

I scrunch my eyebrows. "A hippopotamus?"

"Figure of speech," Lennon says, waving her hand to say, *Let's not get off track.*

"Not one I've ever heard of."

She cocks her hip. "I'll have you know the hippo is the fiercest creature in Africa. Those suckers might look cute and cuddly, but their deadly. Little known fact. For real." I just continue to stare at her. "Anyway, guess what all those things have in common?" She skims over her stupid analogy.

"What?"

"None of those things change whether his last name is Tavern or Cummings." A soft know-it-all smile parts her lips and I hate to admit she's right.

"Even if I wanted him back, I saw the look in his eyes last week. He was done fighting."

"You're wrong. He's not even close to done fighting. He's giving you space. Hoping you'll figure it out for yourself. Go to him." Lennon nudges me like I'm outside his door and too nervous to ring the doorbell.

"I don't even know where he's living . . ."

She tilts her head and her expression says that I'd better come up with a better excuse.

"He could've moved to his family estate or a condo in the city." Lennon doesn't say a word and doesn't move either. "So, he might be at his apartment."

She nods.

"I could try there first?"

She nods again.

"Fine. I'm going." I stand and she smacks my ass.

"Shower first though. Get pretty."

"Um, shouldn't he want to see me even if I'm not dolled up?"

"I'll drive you." She follows me into my bedroom. "The silence thing worked the most, right? I should keep my mouth shut more often."

I roll my eyes and smile even though she can't see me. Appearances can be deceiving. Who would have thought that much wisdom, love and concern would be wrapped up in the crazy, impulsive package that is Lennon?

I THOUGHT ABOUT ALL the different ways this could go down in the shower. Again, I put my life on the line by letting Lennon drive me. She weaves in and out of traffic like we're on the movie set of *Days of Thunder* and she's Tom Cruise.

"Lennon, this isn't the way," I tell her when she bypasses the exit to his place.

"Yeah, I know where he is."

"Where?" I ask, glancing over at her.

"You need to work on your investigative skills." She winks and taps her head with her pointer finger.

"Keep two hands on the wheel, please."

She does a salute and I physically take her hand and place it back on the steering wheel. Her foot presses harder on the accelerator and now we're really flying down the road.

"What's the rush?"

"We can't miss him."

"Where?" I ask, desperate to know what she does.

She glances over at me. "He's boxing."

"So? You don't have to put our lives in danger. We'll catch him." She cringes and I know there's more. "What?"

"He's signing with a promoter who'll move him overseas for a year."

"What?" I screech.

"He said he couldn't stand to be in the same city as you. The thought of running into you with another guy would shred him to pieces. His words, not mine." She gives me a tense smile and glances back at the road.

A hot rush of heat runs through my veins and I suddenly feel nauseated. "What about the merger? The company? Hurry, Lennon," I tell her and she nods her head a few times.

The unicorn van screeches to a halt in front of the white tents and the entire crowd is congregated around one ring, which means he's fighting. I throw the door open, jump over the short fence and push my way through the masses of people.

"Just go, I'll catch up," Lennon screams out but from the swearing going on behind me, I'm fairly sure she's right on my heels, pushing strangers and stepping on their feet.

I finally get to the front of the crowd. The fight has already started, but Lucas isn't in the ring. Turning, I push my way out of the crowd and run toward the table with the brothers. The three are sitting there, drinking quietly, looking at my approach like I'm a crazy person.

"Where's Lucas?" I yell and Sammie cocks his head back. Todd and Derek stare straight ahead.

"He's out," Sammie answers and my heart constricts like someone is squeezing it.

"No." I fall into the chair, my forehead banging on the table with limp arms at my sides. I feel the tears before the first one puddles on the table. Then another one and another. I'm so stupid and stubborn and stupid. How did I let him slip through my fingers?

An arm wraps around my shoulders and Lennon sits next to me, telling me it's going to be okay in my ear.

"I ruined my chance," I mumble.

"Come on. Let's go home." Lennon waits for me to stand and then holds my crumbling body to hers. She helps me to her van and I'm about to climb in when a deep voice rings behind me.

"Can we talk?"

Lennon turns around faster than me, with a look of awe in her eyes. Lucas stands there and the pain inside intensifies knowing I'm too late.

"I'll talk to you in a bit," she says, giving Lucas a quick hug before rounding the hood of the car.

I step away and he leads me down the sidewalk to the spot where he did that first night.

"Kiss and make up," Lennon screams out her window before her tires squeal on the pavement and she and her unicorn van bolt out of the lot.

Lucas chuckles. I really hope this ends well. Otherwise, I'll be bumming a ride home with Sammie.

"Did you lose?" I ask, staring down at my feet shuffling back and forth.

"I didn't fight."

I look up. "Because you're leaving with the promoter. When do you fly out?" I tip my head to wipe the tears from my cheeks as discreetly as possible.

"What?" he asks, his forehead scrunched. "What promoter?"

I glance back to where Lennon was parked. "She said you were signing with a promoter and had to go overseas."

He smiles and rocks back on his heels, shaking his head. "No."

"She said you told her that you couldn't stay in the same city as me. That if you saw me with another guy it'd shred you to pieces." Fucking Lennon.

He steps closer, the heat of his body warming mine. He cups the side of my face, his thumb whisking the tears away.

"True, but I'm not sure I could ever stand to be very far away from you."

My shoulders fall and I close my eyes. Another tear escapes. "I'm sorry," I mumble.

"I didn't catch that," he says, and I stare up at him with tear-filled eyes.

"I'm sorry."

"Again? I must've been hit too many times in the ear."

I punch him lightly in the stomach.

"I love you."

A full-wattage smile consumes his entire face. Oh, boy, I've never seen this particular smile, but I know I want to see more of it. My stomach flutters at the way he's looking at me.

Lucas wraps his arms around me and picks me up so that my feet dangle above the ground. "You're positive you want to bet on me? I'm not the underdog this time." He releases his grip and I slide down his hard body until my feet hit the concrete.

"This time I think I'll go for the sure thing." I slide my hand behind his neck and pull him down to my mouth.

EPILOGUE

"**T**WO BEDROOMS?" I ASK. "Who's sleeping in the other room?"

Lucas has put his boxing gym on hold and has decided to work for Santora-Tavern Sausage and Meats until the merger is complete. He has no plans to stick around but he wants to be sure the company is in good hands so we have something worth leaving *our* kids one day. Cue the swooning, right?

"A roommate." He drops a box onto the kitchen counter and I wait for more information before I go ballistic.

"Roommate?"

"You didn't think I could afford this place on my own, did you?" he asks, unfazed as he unpacks glasses and dishes.

"Yes. I did." I move to the guest room. Vacant. I open up the closet. Nothing.

Two hands wrap around my waist and I swivel around between them to look into his eyes.

"You're joking?"

He chuckles, his head rearing back. "Yes, I'm joking. I was thinking maybe you'd want to keep some of your stuff here."

"In the second bedroom?" I ask, glancing around.

"If that's what you prefer?" He kisses my forehead, releases me and walks back into the kitchen.

"You're allowing me to have a dresser in the second bedroom?" I clarify. Since he only lives three floors up from me, I'm unsure of the point.

Yes, he has decided to not only move to the building where I live, but one-upped me by view and square footage.

He's a jackass, but he's my jackass.

"Yeah," he says and moves to the fridge and cracks open a beer.

"So, tell me." I climb up on the counter and he eases between my legs. I steal the beer from his hands, downing a swig. "Do you pay to be able to go to that speakeasy?" I ask. It's one of the questions that keeps popping up in my head about the time when we were first together.

"I do, yeah."

"Who is Benny?" I ask and he takes the beer to his lips, tilting it back.

"My employee." A smile crosses his lips and I shove him in the chest. He pretends to lose his footing, but comes back to me, dropping the beer on the counter, his hands finding my hips.

"I swear, so many lies," I say, not really upset about the issue. "Makes sense why the waiter was so nervous now." I nod.

"Poor guy. It was his first night and Benny told him who I was." Lucas shakes his head as though he's getting a real kick out of the kid's reaction. "In my defense though, Benny is one of my best childhood friends."

"So, tell me the whole story again," I say and he blows out a breath because I've asked him no fewer than ten times to take me through the time he left his house to now. How he made his money, how he paid for the gym, why boxing and why he's willing to put it on hold.

He kisses my nose. "You have a lifetime to ask me questions and if you knew everything about me right now, what excitement would there be in the future? So, my little OCD preparer, calm down and enjoy our ride." His fingers move to my shirt, unbuttoning the top button.

"Lucas, you have a truck downstairs with boxes and furniture," I remind him, my fingers pushing through his long strands.

"That was all for show. I hired movers." Another button is undone from my shirt.

"What?" I scream and pry his lips off my neck.

"I'm kidding. It only takes me five minutes to ravish your body." He bites his bottom lip and slides me to the edge of the counter.

"Why don't we christen our new bedroom?"

He grabs my ass and I wrap my legs around his waist. "Our?" he asks as he walks us there.

"You don't have to be shy. Go ahead and ask." I smile and he lays me down on the floor.

"These are the rules. One dresser, half a bed, one sink, one chair, we have to share the shower and tub, half the closet. But you can do all the housework and cooking that you want."

"Aw, really? You're so sweet," I say with a saccharine smile.

He nods then laughs. "Keep it coming."

I smack his shoulder. "Ask me for real," I say, my face growing serious as he eases his body over the top of mine.

He leans up and positions himself on his elbow. "Tahlia Santora, will you move in and complain about my dirty clothes on the floor, the crusted dishes in the dishwasher, and my shaving remnants in the sink?" I laugh and shake my head at him, waiting for the serious part to come. "All right. Come on." He stands and holds his hand out for me, then plucks me up off the floor.

He stops me in the kitchen and hands me a small brown box. I open it up and inside there lies the key to his apartment.

"Tahlia, this is your key. I'd like you use it every day and night and I'd really love if it was the only house key on your key ring. But, if you feel it's too soon, then keep it and use it whenever you want. Surprise me." He smiles. "I'd love nothing more than to be here when you get home or vice versa. To have dinner ready for you or vice versa. I want to share every part of my life with you."

I smile, holding the piece of metal in my palm.

"Put those movers on speed dial." I throw myself into his arms and cast kisses all over his face. "They've got an apartment three floors down to pack up." I place a chaste kiss on his lips and then draw back to look at him, my expression serious. "We share all responsibilities except *I* make the coffee."

"Deal." He nods and I hug him tight.

The next morning, we're waiting outside the diner across from Lucas' old apartment with Whitney and Cole.

"This is the place, huh?" Whitney asks, leaning her back on the glass wall, waiting to get in.

"This is it," I answer and we all step forward as the line moves.

"What is it with us and lines?" Lucas's hands wrap around my waist from behind me. He kisses my neck.

"I guess it gives us times to sneak kisses," I respond, turning my head so he can plant one on my lips.

"Where's Lennon?" Cole asks, probably surprised it's only the four of us. She's been our fifth wheel for months now.

"I'm not sure, but I think it's something sketchy," Whitney mentions. "She had the devil in her eyes today."

"You should know, my lead investigative reporter friend." I smile, which only spurs on her happiness about her recent promotion.

"Oh, Tahl told me. Congratulations, Whitney," Lucas adds, his hands never leaving my body. Something I've become addicted to.

"Thanks." She blushes and Cole bends over and kisses her temple, pulling her to his side. "You know, Lucas, you have a lot to celebrate, too."

I stare up at Lucas, admiring him as his face morphs into the epitome of a man who has everything.

"Well, it's been a long road and I'm going to miss boxing, but my body just doesn't heal like it used to. Once everything is sorted out with the sausage company I'll focus on the gym. I think I'd like to expand."

When Lucas put boxing on hold and decided to work for Santora-Tavern Sausage and Meats, to say I was uneasy with it would be a severe understatement. We're taking it one day at a time, but deep down I know he's not Chase. He'll be there for maybe a year and then move on to pursue his passion.

Finally, we're seated and seconds later a cinnamon roll gets placed on our table and we all laugh.

"Are you going to flee now?" Whitney jokes.

"No. I'm not going to flee," I bite out.

"I didn't give her the parting gift this morning." Lucas continues the joke and I narrow my eyes at all of them.

Cole raises his hands. "Hey, I didn't say anything."

I point to him. "You are my only friend at this table."

Whitney slides the cinnamon roll over to her and forks off a huge bite.

"Whit?" Cole questions.

She doesn't even wait to chew and swallow. "I've waited months for them to share this place with me. I've earned first dibs." She forks another piece, swallowing. "Oh, my God, this is so good. You get second, babe." She holds it in front of his mouth and he opens.

Lucas raises his hand for the waitress and a minute later she drops off another one to our table.

"Lucas, these are amazing." Whitney takes another forkful as Cole's eyes glaze over into a sugar coma.

"Thanks, Lucas. I'm going to have to drive down here all the time now," he says.

"No worries, Cole. Lucas will join you." Whitney and I laugh, each digging into our cinnamon rolls.

Both our phones ding at the same time and it's a text from Lennon.

Lennon: HELP! SOS.

Whitney and I look at one another as the two guys talk about baseball or some other sport that I don't follow.

Me: Calm down. What is it?

Lennon: You're never going to believe this.

Whitney: What?

Lennon: Seriously, I thought I could handle anything, but

Me: What?

Whitney: What?

Lennon's text appears on our phones and we both look at one another.

"Oh. My. God," I say and the phone drops from my hands.

"Holy shit," Whitney seconds.

The two guys look over and our phones chime again.

Lennon: See!!! I'm fucked!

The End

Acknowledgements

THANK YOU TIMES A million!

Thank you for betting on the underdog and loving The Bartender, so much, that you carried through to The Boxer. We are grateful to all the bloggers and readers who have reached out to us and shared their love of the characters we adore. We cannot thank all our faithful unicorns enough!

This is kind of like a DITTO to The Bartender, but what can we say, our team worked out so great the first time around, why change. We could not have written this book, or enticed you to one-click it without the following people. Every Piper Rayne team member has contributed to making The Boxer the great read it is.

Djordje Grbic, our Cover Designer

RJ Locksley, our Editor

Behind the Writer, our Proof Reader

Linda Russell, our PR from Sassy Savvy Fabulous

Give Me Books, our promotional company

Blogs, who carved out scheduling time to promote us and/or read and review the book

IndieSage PR—Our Web Designer

Michelle New—Our graphic gal

Type A Formatting—Formatting the paperback

And, of course . . .

we can't forget . . .

because without our other half, there'd be no book . . .

Piper (from Rayne)—for doing half the work.

Rayne (from Piper)—for doing half the work.

Thank you again for all the support on our new venture!

It means the world to us.

 xoxo

 Piper & Rayne

other books by

PIPER RAYNE